SILENCED

WREN'S SONG, BOOK TWO

ADDISON CAIN

1

—————

"She is not to feel pain."

A command like broken glass grinding into an open wound. Sharp, gouging—the kind of abrasive threat that would make a grown man feel Death breathe down his neck.

The physician's hands stuttered, his work dabbing blood from mangled fingers faltering. Such hesitation betrayed much more than the Beta's anxious scent. This was a male who knew one wrong word would see him a corpse. "I'm afraid that is impossible, sir."

Hovering overly close, Caspian snarled. "What did you just say to me?"

In the short minutes since the physician had begun examining his captive mouse, the First Alpha's fine mood had decayed. Raging victory at her chicken-scratched promise of loyalty faded. The glory that had beaten through his chest upon seeing her pale flesh marked by his many bites, depleted.

The ruby-red rivulets of blood that ran from the garish wound where his teeth had pierced her throat were no longer beautiful.

The glassy-eyed albino was a fucking wreck— one stuttering exhale away from the reaper.

Keeping an unwavering eye on his prize, Caspian put a hand on her ankle, one of the few places on her body that was not damaged, as he addressed the frazzled Beta physician who'd been dragged from his bed in the middle of the night.

"*No Pain!* And no scars will remain." This he could give her, stroking his thumb over the protrusion of her ankle bone. "Do you understand me, doc? Only the bite on her neck is to be left alone."

From where he paced beside the bed, Toby issued a challenging growl. Clipped words followed a twitch in his cheek. "My claiming mark will remain on her shoulder, Caspian. Do you hear me? Remove it, and you force me to bite her again."

Chest expanding in an angry breath, Caspian was cut short when the physician interjected. "Gentlemen, I cannot erase this kind of damage with a handheld cauterizing laser. All of these wounds will scar, though I will do my best to keep it minimal. But skin cell manipulation requires delicate application of the larger equipment in my clinic, days of careful monitoring, possible surgery depending on the depth of the damage. She should be brought—"

The very idea inspired pulsating fury in Caspian's chest, a cage of unbending black encasing a shriveled, beating organ. "Suggest taking the Omega from this den again, and I'll slit your throat."

One threat against the old man, and Caspian's mouse finally turned her head. Their eyes met, muddy brown to bloodshot violet, and a look of such heartbreak took her from vacant to wretched. It said, *please*. It urged the target of that glance to settle and be calm.

One thing it did not do was challenge; not that look. The mouse gave him a look of complete and miserable surrender.

Where had the warrior gone? The mouse brave enough to face his brawn with little more than a bent piece of cement-caked rebar?

Where was the hellion who'd taken his leaking cock with a scream, bucking her hips to pull him deeper even as she'd tried to throw him off?

What of the Omega who had set her teeth to his throat, and dared mark him as if she might claim ownership?

How she had howled and spat curses with her eyes. How she'd choked on Toby's then Kieran's cocks, guzzling down their cum once knotted and trapped beneath Caspian's full weight.

He'd filled her to the brim with seed, forced her to hold it all in so it might swim around her belly and let the fiery thing know she was outmanned. And still she'd fought, grinding Caspian's knot deeper, howling her rage as that perfect cunt fluttered and sucked.

Caspian had fucked her every possible way, knotted her more times in those maddening hours than he'd ever taken a woman. It wasn't about keeping her pinned. It was about filling her with more, forcing submission upon the hellcat who had, without question, bruised several of his ribs and torn several pretty gashes into his skin.

The urge to get more cum inside her, to sink his teeth into the wriggling, vicious mouse's flesh... he'd been drunk on it. High on her scent, intoxicated with the strangling grip of her pussy.

On the broken thing's strength.

He'd fucked her face down, scraping her tits over old, wet cement. Flipped her over once the first knot shrunk and shoved his way back in so he might see her blown eyes when he brought her to another ragged climax. All claws and teeth, she'd also taught him that a little Omega severed from sanity was as dangerous as she was fun.

Volleys of blows had struck his temple. But when his little mouse went for the eyes…

Had he been weaker, he would now be blind.

Delicate fists were trapped, but only after she'd broken his nose. Sent him roaring as he knotted her a third time and fucked her into a pulp while his men were in a riot of applause. Hundreds saw. The Syndicate, their slaves… the females daring enough to leave the pen and gawk.

They saw him maul his prize. Saw her disarmed, subdued, and ridden.

And their ovation fed Caspian's beast.

Kieran and Toby savored his kill as well. Just as pack should.

They got the remains the monster within deigned to share.

They got her throat.

The same throat Caspian had torn with his teeth. That *need* had gripped him, demanding all who'd borne witness see that the hissing viper was *his,* no matter whose cock she swallowed.

Kieran had been the one to take her by the hair so Toby's prick could be shoved between her gnashing teeth.

She'd bitten him good, of course. The sick fuck had gotten off on it, cumming almost immediately and swamping her cheeks with spermy cream. Whatever tension had been brewing between Alphas

Two and Three was obliterated when she sputtered and coughed, following that pathetic moment by licking her lips and opening wide for more.

Kieran dipped in, Toby tending to his Second's prostate with a clever finger and words of encouragement.

This was seen by the Syndicate. They saw all three Alphas who ruled them united in victory.

They saw an Omega of amazing capability cowed and owned by her betters.

A glorious, violent mating—truly worthy of his pack.

But even then, the insane little guttersnipe had not submitted. All saw her wriggle her way out of their embrace to seek out a new weapon, and then to scream when the Omega could not find her adopted child.

Before she had been violent. In that instant, she went stark raving mad.

The wiry teenager had been dragged away by wiser members of his gang the moment he'd been stupid enough to beg Caspian for mercy for his *mom*.

Dragged off like the child he was, denied the view of his guardian's interminable and violent rebirth. And that would follow him through the years in the gang.

Once sworn, these males had only one

allegiance.

The Syndicate swore fealty, abandoned family, gave all to their leader.

They didn't cry or beg for mercy.

Alec had failed his first test of loyalty, and would be brutally punished.

He'd missed the glory of the men's cheering— the blood the mouse had drawn from Kieran, Toby, and even Caspian.

In his sobbing state and begging pathetic wailing, he'd missed the glory of an Omega's whirlwind of violence and lust.

God, the pretty mouse's fierce subjugation had been beautiful.

Where she kept that side of herself when mellow and docile, Caspian could never guess. But seeing her unleashed, even just the once, was enough to slake a thirst he'd never known he might possess.

He'd jerk off to the look on her face when he first fucked into her dripping cunt for years. Feel her flesh between his teeth, the taste of her blood and his on his tongue.

The way she'd roared…

But now, after a full and proper capitulation, he did not feel vindicated.

He looked at the little Omega holding his eyes and felt a simmering disquiet.

Damage. Pain. Wounds that would scar.

Broken fingers the best doctor in Dale City was struggling to set.

A female who reeked of loss. Not joy. Not the epiphany of being owned by strong males.

One who suffered.

A grinding, soul-deep moment of realization sunk in. These were not just bite wounds. *Caspian had marked the mouse*. He could still feel the squish of her breaking skin in his teeth, was already eying the unmarked ankle he caressed as if ready to set his teeth to that snowy patch of skin.

And he had chomped down so many times she would be scarred with the crescent shapes of his enthusiasm for life.

Across the bed, Toby continued to pace, no longer replete or satisfied from fucking her mouth. "You should not have threatened her boys."

Drawing up to full height, Caspian cracked his neck and at long last broke the stare he'd shared with the mouse. "Are you not proud of your mate?"

Palms slapping the mattress, rocking it enough that the Omega winced when her body shifted, Toby bellowed, "She's your mate now too! Look at her fucking neck! At her arms, her tits. What part of her did you not maul?"

Only the slender ankle under Caspian's stroking thumb. That was the only place that had somehow been spared in their battle.

A corkscrew of needle sharp sensation rocked Caspian back on his heels, mud brown eyes darting back toward the woman whose gaze was not shut to him. But that was not what held his attention. Bubbling antibiotic foam had been sprayed over the gouges in her neck, dripping a fizzy pink mess down her filthy chest.

Watching it, knowing the reason she bore such wounds, left his overused prick so hard it sawed at the zipper of his pants.

Kieran, arms crossed over a scratched chest, let out the most disappointed of breaths. "You marked her, yes. Get it out of your system before she hits estrous. Fuck her, fill her, knot her, whatever. Then wash your hands of this madness before we lose face."

Toby, veins in his neck throbbing, seethed. "You got hard and marked her with cum, just like the rest of us."

"But I never bit her!" Scrubbing a hand over his jaw, Kieran looked away from his First as if ashamed. "Cunts of all flavors are just down the hall. Females who desire nothing more than to please. You cannot trust one womb! She tried to kill you and you *marked* her for it!"

A hundred women, maybe more, waited in the pen to suck his cock with gusto on demand.

To debase themselves and do filthy things just

for a moment of his attention.

And this mouse was practically a virgin. Unskilled. In no way eager.

Hated him.

And this little slip of girl is the one he'd bonded to in a passion.

Estrous or not, that foreign pining in his chest— the infectious pain—she was the cause!

The Beta doctor cleared his throat, swallowed, and began to set the bones in her other swollen, gnarled hand.

The Omega didn't so much as blink. By all appearances her lavender-rimmed pupils told the story of a bitch in heat. But it was all a lie.

Warm, salty tears marked her blood-speckled cheeks. A deep sense of loss resonated through her spirit straight into Caspian's heart.

His pretty mouse—the utterly still, wrecked girl —grew so far lost in her thoughts, it was as if she didn't notice how the doctor manipulated her joints, the pricks of his needles, or the steady stream of Toby's obnoxiously loud purr.

For all appearances, she felt no physical pain.

But it was a lie. Those violet eyes were clouded by hurt. She even inadvertently shrank when Caspian leaned over her to draw in a long analytical sniff.

He'd threatened the doctor so now she would

not so much as whimper.

Fussing like a smitten schoolgirl, Toby grabbed a discarded pillow and fluffed it, adding it the makeshift nest he'd been building around her for the last hour. All of his efforts smeared with blood and reeking of Omega fear.

Knee to the mattress, he smooshed that pillow into place so she was cocooned in Caspian's bedding, his voice suddenly soft. "There you go, my sunshine."

A bonded male smitten with his mate.

One who practically vibrated with possession.

One who overstepped himself when he grabbed a creamy thigh, gently prying the Omega's legs open. There, for the whole room to see was a cock-battered cunt that still seeped Caspian's seed.

Between pretty, swollen labia oozed a pearlescent trail of male conquering.

Of domination.

As if he had the right, Toby reached forward and scooped up a palm-full of leaking cum. A moment later that same hand was smeared against the gaping wounds on the pretty mouse's neck—rubbed in while Caspian roared.

The Third was flung across the room, Caspian pressing his female down into his mattress. Like a maniac he licked that cum from her wound. Cleaning his mate while offering a comforting purr.

Tongue fully outstretched, he caught himself.

Under him she was utterly still, oddly pliant.

Notched between her bruised thighs, cradled in the shape of her body, Caspian said the words before he could stop himself. "We could come to a compromise, you and I."

Though she seemed asleep, the Omega rattled.

"Show me you're willing to play by my rules, and I'll keep my fierce little mouse."

It wasn't a compromise he sought, no matter the words. He wanted something she was utterly unwilling to offer.

The Omega didn't want him. She didn't want Toby. And Caspian suspected she loathed Kieran. But that thing caging the organs in his ribs hungered for more than her surrender.

"Be a good girl for me until your next estrous. Play house and please. Give me all an Omega owes her Alpha, and I will set your boys free."

For all that she moved, she might as well have been asleep. She judged his word as valueless.

Listing his demands, Caspian began with, "I will fuck other women."

Not so much as a flinch.

Irritated that she believed she could ignore him, Caspian licked at her lips. "Sometimes I'll want those women to fuck you while I watch."

2

———

"**N**o." Wiping blood from his lips, Toby returned to the ailing mouse's side. Voice even, almost conversational despite the reek of rage that wafted from his skin, he said, "Our Omega would not enjoy being used by your sluts. Fuck whoever you want, Caspian, but *my mate* will know only our attention. If you still want Henrietta delivered wearing a big bow, I suggest you honor this stipulation."

Ignoring Toby, Caspian put his nose to the mark that had shredded the Omega's neck, ignoring how she stiffened at the word *mate*. "You will nest in this room."

The Third refused to be unheard. "Caspian, your girls are not to touch her. I'll put down every last bitch in the pen before I allow it!"

Caspian further doled out his commands. "I expect you to smile and purr. Obedience will be rewarded. Defiance will be punished." Hand slipping up her bite-riddled leg, the First Alpha smiled. "You'll see to my cock, to Kieran's, and to Toby's. You will learn to take all three of us at once, dripping pack seed from every last orifice. That is how you shall be paraded before my men."

There it was, a wince. The mouse still had some pride.

"It's up to you, pretty mouse, whether this arrangement lasts a handful of months or a year. The sooner you're healthy enough for estrous, the sooner your boys will be free. Therefore, you will eat what is given. Drink all we offer. You will exercise and dutifully follow the doctor's orders."

A spark began to grow behind the Omega's distance stare. Under weighty distrust, a tiny sliver of hope—just enough to assure her good behavior. Because he knew she no longer had any faith in his empty promises.

People like her survived on belief. And his little mouse was nothing if not a survivor.

One morsel of faith.

A mustard seed.

Careful of her wounds, Caspian climbed off her body, standing over the strange, pale thing. "Alec is to be punished for disloyalty to the Syndicate, pretty mouse. Nothing can be done to change that, but you have ten days to convince me that instead of cutting off his hand, he should only be whipped."

"Be a good girl, and I'll wield the whip myself," Toby crooned, leaning down to press a kiss to her forehead. "I promise it won't be more than a tickle and a little blood for show."

Kieran, still scowling, had his own warning for the Omega. "Toby would also be the one sawing off the dumb kid's hand if you fuck up."

A nod, almost imperceptible, came from the female.

Chest rumbling with the offering of his purr, Caspian smiled. "My pretty little mouse is a good girl. She won't need another reminder."

"No," Toby agreed, another kiss pressed to a snowy head. "She won't."

TWO DAYS REPRIEVE WAS OFFERED. Two days for flesh to heal.

Yet splinted finger bones were weeks from fully mending. She could not talk, not that anyone really wanted to hear her thoughts.

No, they wanted her to smile and sleep, to accept their caresses and food.

The myriad of bites that peppered her flesh were

no longer pink, but slivery scars. They blended in with her skin yet simultaneously stood out like a beacon—shining against powder white.

Glaringly obvious.

A blazing maze that said, *owned.*

Caspian had taken to staring at them, eyes fixed, anytime he was in the room.

That is, when he wasn't touching them, licking them, gnawing over select spots as if to keep his favorites pink enough to stand out.

Her breasts. Her inner thigh.

The only place he treated with true reverence was her ankle.

Toby would fuss over her healing wounds, pouring bitter medicine down her throat. Spoon feeding her. Purring, Caspian had taken to rubbing her feet. All this while Kieran lectured on how she must behave before the men.

While he threatened her Alec. While he pointedly failed to offer more than a passing comment on Mikael's health.

Overindulged as she was, feet dwarfed in callused, careful hands, lips pecked by a smiling shaven-headed psychopath who kept her drugged and buried in pillows, Wren sometimes forgot there was more to notice than lovely sensation and deep, masculine purrs.

Until her fuzzy gaze met disapproving green.

Kieran was an anchor.

One who held himself aloof and stared a great deal.

The behavior of his packmates had the Second Alpha on edge.

Wren could not find it in her to care. Under drugged pain and the itch of mending bone, she felt adrift in her skin. Things weren't right no matter how long the doctor was forced to sit at her bedside.

And forced was the word for it. His life had been threatened in subtle and not so subtle ways those first two days. If she winced, the Beta received a backhand. Should she moan in her sleep, Wren woke to the sound of the doctor being kicked.

"I told you no pain..." Caspian hissed, voice snake-like and deadly.

Worse for wear and smelling unwashed, the older male climbed to his feet and let out a desperate breath. "More drugs will do her more harm than good."

"I don't want her in pain!"

The old man, through exhaustion and days of terror, snapped. "Then you shouldn't have beaten her!"

And that was the last Wren saw of her dedicated caretaker. When she'd woken and found only grinning Toby at her side, she'd vocally cried.

Because she knew what had happened.

The Beta was dead.

And that squishy, invasive comfort streaming through her bones coming from the male shushing and purring at her side...

Mate. Caspian had said.

Flippantly. As if it was nothing of note.

Someone finally wanted her, and he was crazy through and through.

Signing poorly, he talked as he practiced structuring her language. "Sunshine. You're looking much better today."

Unable to converse with her fingers still splinted, Wren only blinked.

"Are you hungry?" That sign he had down pat.

No.

"Thirsty?"

No.

Face thoughtful, an uncharacteristic scowl came to Toby's brow. "I've waited a long time for you. For my mate."

It took everything an exhausted Wren had not to show an ounce of disappointment.

"I know this is new. An adjustment period is to be expected." A wink brought out fine lines on the side of Toby's eyes. Laying on the charm, he said, "A month from now you'll be so in love with me you'll never remember that it started... with difficulty."

She felt her brow arch before she realized she'd done it.

Chuckling, purr amplified as he leaned over, Toby grinned. "Trust me, sunshine."

Wren trusted a burning building more than the madman with his dangerous fetishes.

"I'll learn how to love you however you like best. You have my word on that, Jax. I'll buy you pretty baubles, give you pretty dresses, and feed you all the water a girl could want."

On and on went the diatribe, Wren's eyes growing heavy. When well-muscled arms snuck around her and a shamefully misbuilt nest buckled under the Third Alpha's weight, she slept.

That is until Caspian barged in, dragging Rosie behind him. "Get out. Your time with her is over."

3

____

Red lips painted to perfection, dressed in blue to bring out her eyes.

Rosie.

Perfect and pretty and not at all scarred.

Rosie, who didn't bear the mark for *defective* upon her face.

Weight in the nest shifting at her back, Toby rolled his shoulders, stretching from his nap. All of it for show, Wren could sense that bone deep.

With a wink and a quick stolen kiss on parted lips, the dismissed Third Alpha said, "Be my sweet sunshine for Caspian." In a snap, his gaze turned toward the couple at the door, all semblance of gentleness replaced with a murderous sneer. Voice loud enough to assure every word was heard, he announced, "And if Rosie touches you, I'll kill her. It won't be quick."

Graceful, hazarding on careless, Toby climbed from the nest, heading out the door with no further word. Not even a glance at his scowling leader.

Nor did he so much as twitch at the snarled, "Later," that came from his First.

The first thing someone learned upon being thrust into the Warrens was that bad things would always get worse. If you starved so hard your belly protruded, the next thing you knew, your first meal would give you dysentery. Many died this way.

Those who grew so thirsty they drank from the puddles knew the microbes would rot their teeth. What could be worse?

It would also rot them from the inside out.

Decaying that way took time… and led to an ugly death.

A female might be captured and forcibly mated. Perhaps three of them took her, used her, and toyed with her future for sport. Out of estrous they might mark her. They might threaten her family. They might break her and pretend at putting her back together.

They might contaminate unwelcome bonds that rattled bones and made her innards ache.

They might insult her by bringing in a more adequate female. By fucking her in front of them.

Reminding the Warrens rat that, claiming marks or no, she was nothing… and that it could always get worse.

Perhaps this knowledge was why Wren didn't blink, expected nothing but ugliness from these males.

No matter Caspian's promises, they would not keep Alec safe. But that didn't mean she refused to play their game and put him in direct harm either.

Heal, earn their trust, flee.

Take her boys, sell her body along the monorail tracks to get them all out of Dale City. Steal if she had to. Run so far Caspian could never find them.

But these things took time. So for now, Wren sat up, the soft blanket Toby had used to cover her nakedness falling away to show bite-marked breasts. Each little matching crescent had almost healed thanks to the doctor's advanced tech, his diligence, and his forced captivity it this room.

And he had been murdered for it. Wren didn't doubt that for a minute.

He had been murdered because she'd slipped. A single errant whimper, that is what his life had been worth.

She wouldn't slip again.

These men wanted to play house? Fine, she'd be their pretty mouse, their sunshine, their whore.

She'd eat their food, drink their water, take their

medicine and grow strong. Eyes glowing with intention, Wren met the muddy gaze of a very bad man.

One look, and Caspian make a hungry sound, one so desperate she almost thought she'd heard him whine.

And maybe he did. Rosie certainly turned his way, an incredulous look on her perfect face.

"You've eaten today?"

Two bowls of the green goo, yes.

"Drank plenty of water?"

So much that Wren felt bloated and was annoyed by the near constant urge to pee.

"Are you in pain?"

So much fucking pain she hardly knew how to force the simple head shake of *no*.

Her nailbeds, though coated in scabs, stung. Her broken fingers itched and ached. Her skin had been sealed on the surface, thanks to the kind Beta doctor, but deeper wounds, all the bruising, were days away from anything but leaving her a pulped mass of aches.

Worse than all the physical ailments was the unseen one. The bone-deep internal twitch that was Toby's crudely forged link. The buzzing pinching of her internal organs marked Caspian's cruelty and connection.

The pair of them had infested her living corpse.

And they would be the death of her. But not

until she got her boys as fucking far away as possible. She'd even kill them if that's what it came down to.

But not in a rage. They were too strong for even that mindless death-machine Omegas became to protect their brood. They were the perfect pack, despite their grievances and constant snarling back and forth.

Hand to his throat, Caspian kneaded the skin as if unaware of what he was doing. "You don't seem well."

Splinted fingers did a poor job of trying to smooth bed-wild hair into something fetching.

"I've waited two days, and I need to fuck." This all blurted out while the obvious erection in Caspian's pants leaked.

Then fuck Rosie, Wren thought. Glad he was far enough away that his poor excuse of a purr couldn't truly touch her.

Utter filth, the Alpha's eyes glowed with something perverse. "But I want to look at you while I'm doing it."

Relief faintly coursed through tired veins.

As if he too felt his offer was her balm, Caspian drew his hands from a throat grown red from rubbing to knock against his heart. Or perhaps she misread him, for his grimace made it seem as if the last batch of food stuffed down his maw must pain him.

Dragging a silent, yet strangely composed Rosie behind him, the First Alpha approached. "Scoot to the edge of the bed, pretty mouse. Spread your legs so I can see your juicy cunt."

The only part of her that didn't ache.

Fine.

Hair a tangled mess, unwashed and a physical wreck, Wren slunk to the edge, laid back even as Caspian pulled out his cock, and locked her eyes on the water-stained ceiling.

A sound of distress came from the beautiful blonde in the pretty blue dress. It was not the sound of a woman getting fucked, it was the sound of a person shoved to their knees then choked on a fleshy length of meat.

And it was enough to draw lavender eyes from the uneven ceiling to the eyes of her living, breathing tormentor.

He looked as if he suffered the most terrible kind of pain.

Staring down between her legs. To the dry slit. To pink inner labia that fanned out from chalk-white skin. To the cunt he'd previously penetrated, filled with filthy cum, and tasted.

And for some unknown reason, knowing he was skull fucking another woman, and staring at a thing he would not let himself have, Wren almost felt sorry for him. Which made little sense, considering the man had no real regard for her welfare beyond that of a favored toy. Knowing that the marks he'd left on her would prove this whole thing pointless.

She felt sorry as he did things to Rosie's throat that would have made Wren vomit.

She felt sorry that no matter how often or hard he fucked his favorite Omega, he'd never know joy.

She felt sorry that she hated his guts and wished to see him destroyed.

And she felt sorry that she grew wet to the sounds of another woman gagging on his cock.

One tiny pearl of slick, that was all it took to shatter Caspian's composure.

One second he had been little more than a perverted voyeur. The next he buckled over and set his mouth to the very part of her he'd demolished two days prior.

Lapping at her like a madman. Trying to drink up the sad offering a disinterested body might offer. He growled, whined like a dog, then rested his head on her sunken belly as he gushed his seed down the throat of another.

None of it had been for Wren's pleasure. No, he'd swallowed her up in greed.

But as the male panted, bent over, rubbing his

scruffy face on her belly, she took pity and stroked his head with splinted hands.

"You need to eat more, pretty mouse…"

Softly spoken words that made no sense.

Lavender eyes drew down just in time to see small, female hands grasp Caspian's knot and massage it in a way that would milk him almost like a cunt. She saw the wheat colored hair peeking up from the edge of the bed she'd been forced to "nest" in. She saw the travesty this would be if she'd loved this male.

But she didn't.

And she didn't care.

That did not stop her gasp when Caspian stopped licking her for his pleasure and doubled down his effort for hers. Light airy flicks over her clit, swirling, pointed laps of a tongue over labia and slit.

It should have been humiliating how quickly she came. Her empty cunt flooded with slick so quickly the room spun. It drenched his face and set the Alpha into a fit of long groans.

"Thank you."

What the actual fuck?

Kicking back, scooting away from the mouth on her parts, Wren needed to be anywhere but this room. As far as possible from an existence where a shrinking penis was slipping from the loudly sucking lips of a foreign woman.

She needed to be home, in her beloved nest, surrounded by her boys and salvage.

"Shhhhhhhhh, darling mouse." Soft kisses came over deep scattered wounds that ached the most. "Be still, I don't want to hurt you. I'll fuck this sweet pussy as soon as you might handle me. I'll fuck you so hard you'll forget your name."

Coughing up the excess cum that had overcome her throat, Rosie wiped at her running mascara.

Her face red, blue eyes on the cracked cement floor she stood, straightening her dress and smoothing her hair as if this horrible treatment meant nothing to her.

It wasn't just Wren who'd been degraded.

And that, that is what broke a bitter Omega's heart.

4

———————

"Mmmhh." Drugged by deep sleep, a breathy hmmm escaped Wren's parted lips.

A rocking sensation drew her further from muddled dreams—a gentle bump, bump, bump that jostled just enough a sleepy Wren's lashes parted. She nearly gasped.

Kieran.

At her side, braced, the naked beauty of the only Alpha male who'd yet to intrude into her *nest*.

Not quite near enough to touch, not even looking at her in the dark. His sculpted body—defined muscles rippling—caught up in pleasure.

But it was *why* muffled grunts were kept locked behind his teeth that left her frozen still.

Fists clenched in the covers, sweat gathered on Kieran's brow.

He was being fucked… by a softly whispering Toby. "Look how pretty she is, our sweet Omega. Smell her eager cunt. Fill her up with a feast for me."

One word grunted impatiently passed Kieran's parted lips. "Harder."

To hear him breathless, to see him mounted by a lower ranked Alpha… for pleasure… Wren didn't know what to make of it.

What had been rolling hips, Toby hardly visible in the dark, became rough, dedicated thrusts that jostled both bodies closer to where she laid. Shrouded in shadows, Wren spied from slightly parted lids, and saw little of Toby's naked form beyond where his hands stroked Kieran's back, or where his pelvis shoved a lube shined cock straight into the Alpha's body. But she sensed through their link that he was fully aware of her regard.

And was pleased by it.

She could even feel his pleasure, his building release in the base of her spine.

She could hear him silently calling to her, tempting her to be braver and show them her attention.

That was his game.

And where she refused to engage, the bed began

to shake with more force, knocking back against the wall so roughly that there was no way she could pretend to be asleep.

Caspian's massive form was pressed to her back. Unsure if he slept or if he too had his eyes on the scene, Wren had her answer a moment later.

He gave an approving grunt right before something thick and wriggling borrowed between her thighs.

Fingers.

They slipped and danced as her clit peeked from its hood and her labia bloomed with unexpected slick.

There was no hiding her response. For the first time in the presence of these men, Wren was aroused by something other than an Alpha growl, desire perfuming the air with the scent of honest slick.

Hooking his fingers behind her pelvic bone, Caspian rubbed hard at that secret spot. Teasing the nerves, milking her slick glands until a wet squelch of noise squished with his hands' every movement.

She should have been scandalized at the taboo scene taking place beside her, not readily spilling slick.

She should have shut her eyes so hard she'd never have to see Kieran's pupils expand when he got the first breath of her arousal.

She should not have moaned when Caspian began to thrust his slippery fingers in and out of her hungry hole in tempo with Toby's cock disappearing into Kieran's ass.

And she definitely should not have looked to see the engorged prick hanging down from Kieran's hips, dragging a trail of precum over the sheets.

She'd never seen his dick so big. So angry looking.

Face almost hostile in its hopeless pleasure, Wren couldn't deny this act was something the Second Alpha enjoyed.

Not when his fat cock rocked back and forth with the swing of Toby's hips, a pendulum that left her mouth watering. Kieran was uncut, the swollen head having burst past his foreskin to shine as it dripped beads of delicious fluid.

Unsure what drove her, Wren desired to reach out and suck that dangling organ. To wrap her hands around the hint of his knot just as she'd watched Rosie do to Caspian the last several days.

More slick gushed from her slit.

Toby fucking Kieran before her eyes. The daily display of Caspian sitting in his chair, staring at Wren's naked body—staring into her eyes—while Rosie labored to suck him dry. Rosie who may as well not have been there for all the heed he paid her. She was a hole, one he could use while his mouse was still in too much pain to bear his sexual aggression.

These thoughts blended into one pornographic mess, stirred up her sleep-labored brain into a whirlwind of carnal craving that hit Wren like a punch in the gut.

With a strangled cry, she gushed all over Caspian's hands, her leg shaking when she kicked and cried out a disgusting release.

"Naughty girl, I didn't say this pretty pussy could cum." Grainy, his voice slurred with desire, Caspian whispered equal parts chastisement and filthy praise in her ear. "Now you'll have to be punished."

With mouth and hand.

Teeth took to her shoulder, biting down with enough force that she hissed. Where his calloused hand forcibly moved between her thighs, Caspian increased the pressure and speed of his fingers, fucking into her so hard slick squirt out and sprayed her legs.

Where was her blanket?

Why couldn't she think straight?

And *why* didn't she protest when Kieran reached for her, flopping her around like a rag doll and dragging her under his rocking body?

One moment she'd been flush with Caspian, a

second later she was spread-eagle, prone directly under Kieran's pulsating cock.

Impaled without so much as a kiss or sweet word, that instrument burrowed its way deep.

Though it had only been days since she'd been filled, the burn and stretch reminded her so much of that first time Caspian had mounted her in her home that Wren could almost smell the mildew dank air.

Home…

A smile bloomed on her lips.

And then Toby drove all three of them forward.

"Fuck!" Kieran lowed as the veins in his neck pulsed.

Toby made his own animal sounds and he reached past the man who sheathed his dick and fisted a handful of Wren's hair. "Look at her, Kieran! Tell me there is not a more beautiful female on this planet!"

Hooded eyes, mouth slack from over-sensation, Kieran seemed beyond anything but the feel of squeezing cunt and invasive cock.

Already knotting her, Wren's needy pussy fluttered in protest as the bulge of flesh grew too large to give her the friction a starved womb desired.

Still she came, her body unable to deny such pressure, or to deny the chance to feed off warm, soupy cum that dumped from the beautiful male straight into her.

Toby, however, was not yet ready to release.

As if to punish the Second for such selfishness, or as if to laud him for swelling the Omega's belly with so much sperm, Toby began an all-out assault on Kieran's ass.

Tied to her by his knot, there was nothing the Second could do to stop him. Though he snarled, and threw back his head with threats of death, dismemberment, revenge…

Through it all, Toby laughed.

Until he too was swept away, breath caught in a grunt, face twisted as he jetted the Second full of his first burst of cum.

Pulling out, spraying over Kieran's back, Wren's face, her nest… everywhere.

The force with which creamy fluid shot out of him, the way he continued to beat at his throbbing meat and mangle his knot. Wren had never seen anything like it.

Testicles drew up tight, swelled, shrank, swelled. Over and over like a living thing. A fountain of cum that speckled his pecs, ran dripping down his straining thighs.

As his usherings wound down, a panting Toby announced to the Alpha who'd yet to fully partici-pate. "She still wants more."

With a grunt of agreement, Caspian shifted his

weight. "I feel it too. Our pretty cum-slut doesn't think one knot is enough."

Tawny hair hanging in his eyes, the tips spiky with sweat, Kieran hoisted a stiffening Wren upright.

"Don't be nervous. Shhhhh," Caspian whispered, his chest sliding over her back. "This one time, I'll go easy on you."

Cockhead to her second hole, pressing forward before she'd grasped what this was, Wren clung to Kieran, her splints digging into his back as her asshole was breached.

It hurt, gravity pulling her down Caspian's aching organ.

She could sense his impatience, how much he needed friction to alleviate a pain he'd been carrying in his cock for days.

No amount of Rosie's mouth had fully satisfied him.

Not one of the cunts he'd used in the pen where Wren couldn't see.

He'd been a walking, disgruntled erection.

His knots has been insignificant, the usherings he'd poured in his women meager.

The tight ring of her ass squeezed him so tight, her guts *felt* his pleasure.

Perverse groans vibrated from him to her. They

echoed through the bones Toby had claimed, left her resonating with *them*.

One sated. One in desperate need.

And her trapped in pleasure and pain—realizing that this whole event had been staged.

Kieran's knot gave a mighty pulse, he emptied another great spurt just as Caspian found himself fully seated. There was only a small bit of flesh between their cocks, and she was such a small girl to be speared so relentlessly.

Sweating from the urge to force them both out, head lolling back against the First Alpha who *always* took advantage, Wren felt a sweat drip down her temple.

Toby kissed it away. Just as he murmured words of encouragement and love to her when Caspian began to thrust.

There was slick enough to smooth Caspian's invasion. There was cum enough still pouring from Kieran to keep Wren's cunt contracting. And there was Toby incessant kisses on her mouth, his breath mingling with hers until all three of them filled her up.

The orgasm that twisted from her toes and locked each muscle up tight, left her screaming like a woman caught under the knife. Any who heard would have thought they'd tortured her. Beat her. Broke her down bit by bit.

They would have seen the grimace that rode those cries, and not known it for what it was.

Matching the intensity of her dirge, Caspian erupted. A volley of warmth shot so deep inside her the sensation would never fade. He came, his knot outside her tender ring, yet threatening the gate.

He came.

And so did she.

As if it was the first time, ever.

And when it was over? When the men gently disengaged and a flood of their seed dumped from her cunt and ass? When she had to sit in the mess and realize that she was awake, that this *thing* had happened between them. That she still thrummed with their pleasure and completion?

Wren sat dumbstruck.

5

I t was Toby's voice that finally broke through the ringing in her head. "You're okay, sunshine."

Okay?

"Come here."

As in move? No. She couldn't do that. Everything was still buzzing, swirling, and pinching under her skin. A flood still leaked out of her, staining her legs with slippery scented ownership.

And this room smelled terrible.

Like other women. Like years of sex, and pain, and… *Longing?*

Help.

Wren wanted to shout out that word. But she'd never been able to speak. No matter how many times her father had slapped her for willfully remaining silent. No matter how much her flustered mother had begged.

Help me.

Fingers threaded through her hair, kneading a head grown cottony. "I'm here, sunshine."

My nest is all wrong. This room is too dark. My chest hurts. I'm frightened!

"Let's get you cleaned up, hmmm?"

I'm drowning. You're killing me.

"There's nothing like a bath after a hard fuck up the ass, eh, Kieran?" A good natured slap bounded off the lolling Second's ass.

Rolling back, arm thrown over his handsome face, Kieran growled a spent, "I'm going to castrate you with a rusty spoon."

How could this be nothing to them? How could they tangle their limbs with hers and press their heated flesh to her body as if ready to find slumber in the cooling pools of their shared ejaculate?

"Up you go." Arms came under knees, cradled her shoulders, and Wren was carried away from the scene of her destruction.

"When you look at me with those big eyes, I know you can see me." Toby nuzzled her nose with his. "A little fear, a little wonder… Someday you'll even learn to smile. And it won't be from the gifts, or the fucking, or the babies that will swell out your belly. It will be because you just can't help yourself, sweet pea." With a chuckle, he added, "Well, some of those grins will be from the fucking. I'm going to keep you so clogged with cum that it will never stop dripping from those fleshy little petals between your legs. Everyone will know I was Alpha enough to claim a mate."

With the heat in his last words, the snarling challenge as he bit out each syllable, Wren grew smaller.

Alphas didn't claim mates unless they wanted to breed, or were growing old and wanted the constant companionship of a bonded female slave. Young males, men of power, would never!

Yet Toby had bitten her. Purposefully, brutally. And, stupid as Wren was, she had not realized it until after she'd faced the three of them down in the Waterworks.

And lost.

Caspian had done far more than bitten her. He'd mauled her flesh, scarring her for life on every last place anyone might see.

Except her face. That had already been ruined by the tattoo that marked her as defective.

But at least Caspian had also said his claim would only last until her Estrous. It almost made this madness seem reasonable. But Toby, he wanted to *keep* her.

Yet he let the others have their fun. Built a

malformed nest around her and played on her fears for his benefit.

A good mate would bring her her boys.

A good mate wouldn't have seen her ripped from her home and degraded.

Good mates did not exist.

And that horrible truth was something all Omegas learned young.

Having missed the sound of water filling the tub, Wren hissed when the thing she'd been clinging to lowered her down. A drowned Warrens rat swimming in a pool of fluids, and pain, and inner disgust.

Help me.

Those two words would never be heeded in a place like this.

He took a cup and poured water over her unwashed hair. "I promise you everything is going to be okay."

No. It wouldn't be.

Suds were added, all those dingy locks washed clean until they sparkled like fresh snow.

Wren had never seen snow. Only mud and dirty air and disappointment.

"Dip your head back. Good." Male hands worked under the water, her hair floating behind her like the net she'd been caught in. "I knew you'd do me proud tonight. When tempted, Kieran has never been able to resist you. Do you know why?"

Kieran is a horrible male.

"Because for as far back as he can remember, his mother pimped him out so she could get a fix."

A drop, a sinking hold of sensation, sucked the air from lifeless lungs.

Toby winked, still toying with her hair under the water. "Mommy issues galore. And then there you are, offering your life for two kids who aren't even yours."

Oh, they were hers. In every possible fucking way but DNA, those boys were hers. And that right there was the reminder she needed to pull herself out of the tornado of ugliness these males had trapped her in tonight.

A full breath stretched her ribs.

"So you understand?" Helping her sit up, Toby reached for a bottle of scentless cream that would keep her hair soft and shining. "No one has ever loved him. I certainly don't. Caspian hates him. But you can. You will."

No.

"Yes, you will. You'll love him for all the times he was forced to take a cock so his mom might get high. You'll love the little boy who never had a soul to kiss his scraped knees. You'll love him because you know exactly why he is the way he is." Again he pushed her back into the water to rinse silken hair clean. "Granted, you might die the death of one-thousand cuts along the way… but I'll be here to lick your wounds clean."

I'm going to take my boys far away from you. From all of you.

"And Caspian, he's completely under your spell. Won't it be fun to watch him falter and break?"

You're a sick man.

"That's enough of a soak for my sweet little sunshine. Come on out now." Water sloshed, spilling from the tub to rush over cracked tiles, Wren pulled from enough water to hydrate a family for a week. "Let's dry your splints and make sure the swelling's in check. Then straight back to bed with you."

6

———

Wren was restless. A good sign that healing progressed, that pneumonia retreated, and that Alec's ten days were almost up.

Funny how ten days could pass in a blur.

When they weren't fucking her, one of them was sleeping beside her—as if they managed their criminal syndicate in shifts.—leaving her trapped in the most disgusting nest imaginable.

It was filthy, the bedding having not been changed since the day she'd signed her soul away to Caspian. And it seemed the males didn't mind the bloodstains, or dried salves, or the days' worth of sexual fluids that had soaked so deep that entire blankets were stiff and crunched when moved.

In fact, it seemed they were competing to see who could defile her nesting place the most.

It was hard to judge the winner.

Kieran certainly sprayed more cum than the others—pointedly directing his eruptions to all corners like a dog marking his territory. After he'd pounded her down into the bedding, that first knot was always wasted, left to splatter her breasts so he could use the whole of his body to rub his scent all over her flesh when he fucked her immediately after the last salty droplet splashed her skin. He used her roughly, forcibly ensuring her pleasure under extreme circumstances and chastising if she failed to cum.

The Second rarely slept, using his time with their broken captive to play every sick sort of sexual game he might imagine. This he did, Wren was certain, in an attempt to make her balk. He wanted her to fail.

He wanted her gone.

Yet clung to her in the rare moments his exhausted eyes did close.

When he'd wake, untangle his limbs, hand running through his dark hair as he stood over her, he'd scowl. And then she'd be punished with words —all the ways the other whores sucked cock better. That she was sickly and weak… an embarrassment.

His tirade never took place before the other

males. No, it was Kieran's secret spite and blatant insecurity that stabbed at her in exactly the right place. Because all he claimed was true.

Wren could hardly take a cock down her throat without gagging and begging for air. She didn't know advanced sexual technique, or exotic positions. And yes, she was ill, and scarred, and had lived her entire life aware her defects made her an embarrassment.

So the barbs didn't sting her already numbed psyche, and that frustrated Kieran all the more.

The Second Alpha was not going to inspire the meltdown they both knew he hoped would get her sent from Caspian's den.

Yet still he pushed. He'd ask her to bend backwards like a bridge and bear the entire weight of her inverted body on hands and feet so he could fuck her until her legs cramped and she fell. She'd obey, the upside-down world rocking as her hair brushed the floor.

When inevitable failure to hold such a position brought her tumbling to the ground, again he'd compare her to all the beauty that waited in the pen. Yet it wasn't them who'd pull his head to her breast, and comb through those tawny locks with her fingers while he sputtered and raged… and allowed it.

The dark marks under his eyes, the obvious

exhaustion. He became putty—that slept and drooled and clung so hard it made her bones ache until the cycle could repeat.

Then there was Toby who thought he was her succor. Toby who saw that she was gently bathed, that her hair was combed, medicines injected and swallowed, fingers observed. Toby who talked to her with his hands as he practiced sign language. Toby who would devour the pussy Kieran inevitably left stuffed with his cum for hours on end.

Until her nerves couldn't take another second.

Until she truly wanted to scream.

It was his attention that sent her closest to falling off the edge. Toby's *dedication* that endangered Alec.

Because she wanted to slap him away and scream that she didn't need his tenderness or pretty words.

Were Kieran wiser, he'd forfeit his time and give Toby every possible hour to drive her insane.

"You look much better today. Rosy cheeked and soft as silk." He'd signed it perfectly.

A small, practiced smile was offered. Wren playing house, playing mate, to appease the one whose bond rattled in her bones with unmatched hunger.

"Once your cough is under control, and your lungs have recovered, I'll take you up top to a restaurant and a show. Just us two for a night on the town."

Like normal women who didn't sleep in filth and sell their bodies? Air left her lungs, a slight disbelieving snort ruining Wren's facade.

Tone edging toward warning, Toby said. "All other males will envy me."

Resolute energy flowed from his end of the bond, the buzz working to chase away her incredulity.

The life he'd paint for her... how many years had she dreamed of such things? It was as if he plucked the thoughts out of her head and offered them to her on a silver platter.

But all that sparkled in his display was poisoned. And she knew that.

Knew better.

Because there were no decent Alphas.

And she would never get to go up top. Never sit at a fancy restaurant's table. Never smile while draped in diamonds.

But Toby in his unintentional cruelty was also relentless.

Once when she was still aching from Kieran's attention, when she was tired and frightened and lonely for her boys, Toby's ministrations and his measured promises of the perfect life cracked her armor.

Wren had cried.

Toby had seen it.

But instead of raging at her for breaking character, he set the brush aside and pulled her to his chest.

Purring, he let her splinter, felt her desolation through the tenuous link, and did nothing more than hold her.

More importantly, when she was finished and shaking, scared for what she'd done, he promised not to tell.

Caspian and Kieran didn't need to know.

But the First Alpha had felt her wretchedness through the link, and came in a high temper to see what had happened. By then, Toby had dried her eyes, kissed her lips swollen and pink, and left her exactly the way Caspian liked to see her best.

Clean. Virginal.

Shy.

Nervous.

The distraction slowed Caspian's angry breath.

With a stroke down her smoothed hair, Toby said, "It was a coughing fit. Nothing more."

"She's supposed to be getting better!" The First Alpha paced the length of his room, openly angry at the intangible thing that kept her chest ratting despite breathing treatments, special food, and a smorgasbord of pharmaceuticals.

Truthfully, Wren was.

Though her chest still ached, she could draw in a deeper breath than she had been able to in years. In the last ten days, her body had begun to fill out, breasts ripening and rear getting plump. She'd always been extremely pale, but now her skin was no longer sallow and sunken.

There was still ample mending to be done, but her health was much improved, considering…

For the first time in years, she was actually *sick* of a eating the same thing day in and day out. A luxury of feeling only the well-fed might ever know.

"Well, I'll leave you to it." Toby pressed a lingering kiss to her forehead. "Be a good girl, sunshine. Caspian's had a hard day."

Caspian… who brought his other whores to the den she nested in. Who would barge in and throw back her covers, so he might reach for and stroke her ankle while he looked her over every single morning.

Whatever he saw determined which woman he'd summon to service him.

Usually it was Rosie, days on her knees having left their mark in rug burn and scrapes. But Wren had also seen a lovely black-haired doll. A red-head with smiling lips and a vacant expression. And others who'd faded into the background.

Some arrived obviously high, eyes half-lidded and swaying on their feet. Some came reeking of perfume, their clothing already mussed from another male's use.

Not a single one of them looked at Wren, as if ordered to ignore the mangled Omega and her mockery of a nest.

But Rosie, she always snuck a glance when Caspian wasn't looking.

Usually after the First Alpha had sent her sprawling with a shove, and stood over his healing prize, splashing the jets of warm cum Rosie's hard work had inspired over Wren's bared tits and cunt.

Zipping up, he'd leave Wren coated in seed, ignoring where Rosie gathered herself from the floor, and went about his business.

Until his cock would grow hard again, and Rosie, *again*, would be ordered to her knees to drain him. Sometimes he bent the blonde over in half, ass up at the edge of the bed so Caspian's mouth could sample the delights of his caught prize while he fucked a pussy he could pound with all the violent enthusiasm Wren knew he wanted to pour upon her.

She wondered why he even bothered to play a game that clearly made him miserable.

When all three of the males gathered nightly to share her as one, the trio were savage, snapping teeth and guttural grunts. It was only in these private moments Caspian seemed cautious.

After hours of this charade, after he'd fumbled

through papers and worked via the data relay on his arm, the flavor-of-the-day would be ordered away with a blunt, "Get out," and only when they were alone, would Caspian creep into Wren's nest.

The cock that had been in another woman's mouth or pussy would then be buried between her thighs, the brutal First Alpha struggling to take her as gently as a barbarian might. When he knotted, felt her traitorous cunt's pulsating and eager response, a low whine always intermingled within his moans.

Only once he'd done this, forgetting Rosie was still in the room.

The blonde Omega had watched the entire exchange, her face blank of all emotion. When Caspian's knot had subsided, when he'd kissed the back of Wren's neck, licked at the scars he'd left on her throat, and praised her with the filthiest words he might find, he left the nest to take a piss.

His eyes had caught on Rosie.

The look he'd given her was... callous.

As if she were as insignificant as an empty dish, he continued forward and left the women alone together for the brief time it would take to drain his bladder.

"Monsters, all of them." Hard words from a hard woman, Rosie slicing through Wren with a razor sharp gaze. "Wipe that look off your face. Never let an Alpha see."

The look in question was shame. Wren was inundated with it.

For coming so hard the world had gone fuzzy. For mewing and urging the male who'd just used another woman to show her his physical affections. For wanting the woman who had pleasured him with her mouth for hours to see that it was really her cunt he craved. For debasing herself. For enjoying it. For being a petty bitch who was so fucking riddled with secret jealousy she wanted to tear every woman who'd known Caspian's attention limb from limb. Who knew that such thoughts were evil and tried to stuff them down so far she felt nothing, saw nothing, but the way he looked at her as he used them.

Who was slowly going insane with worry for her boys.

And whose fingers were still trapped in splints. Who was silent and anxious, yet still got wet when the First Alpha gave her *that* look.

Pouring a glass of water, Rosie brought it over and held it to Wren's mouth. "We'll never be friends. Don't look to me for help."

The door opened, Toby walking it to find Rosie at his mate's bedside.

Before he might reach over and snap her neck, Rosie said, "Your Omega can't properly nest under these conditions. This bedding is filthy. The mattress reeks of other women. Take better care of your things or put her in the pen where she can take care of herself."

And like a truly uppity bitch, she tossed her blonde hair, and walk right past the seething male.

Within the hour, the mattress, pillows, blankets, all of it, had been carted away and replaced with new. Toby, with Caspian lingering near his work, stood by and watched Wren build a real nest. Both of them leaning on their portion of the link—aware that despite her blank expression, she was elated to be free of the horrible smell.

The new nest was the finest she'd ever built.

7
____

These sensations, inside and out, were entirely fresh. Even the pitch of her purr was on a scale Wren couldn't recall having producing before. Lush and indulgent, it hummed from her chest while she let herself do something as silly as burrow.

As if she were happy—safe, and separated from the nightmare of her life.

Cocooned in snowy white cotton, weighted down with blankets stuffed with fluff, she allowed herself a moment of bliss.

In a nest.

A perfect nest made from wonderful things.

Yet the precious moment ended when a warm hand reached under impeccably arranged covers to seize her ankle.

Purr stuttering to a complete stop, Wren braced, found her heart beat far too fast, and forced out a different purr. *The expected purr.*

"It's rude not to invite me in, mouse." The male teased. "And what happens to bad girls?"

They get fucked. Hard. Without the growl or sweet lies.

They get shown that they like it.

Reminded they were made to be a whore.

Yet, it was the little moments, Wren reminded herself. The little moments hidden within the bad one had to treasure. And even though it had been short-lived, she had enjoyed her fresh nest while it had really been hers.

Would dream of it. Hold it in her mind just as it was now.

Before they spoiled it.

Pulling her leg from Caspian's grip, Wren maneuvered like a fish in water. The bedding above her peaked as she flipped. Where his hand waited, her face appeared.

A little mouse peeking out of her hole.

Because she could not bring herself to reach for him, Wren looked to his fingers. Veined and rough, she set her teeth to a knuckle and bit down hard enough to sting. Leading a chuckling monster in as if carrying a kitten in her teeth, Wren brought Caspian into a sacred Omega space.

It seemed the male would pretend respect. He didn't immediately make a grab for her breasts or shove his thick fingers in her cunt. Instead he settled exactly where he should.

He rested, pulling her weight into the nook at his side.

Looking down at the intruder, blankets tented by her head, she blinked.

The man just lay there; arm behind his head, eyes closed.

A moment later, it seemed he snored.

Slinking from his chest, Wren went back to her secret preening, her rolling about, and her sighs— finding that the scent of an Alpha had only enhanced the comfort found in soft sheets.

Even if the Alpha was Caspian.

Her natural purr returned, there was even a soft smile playing at her lips with so much clean slipping against her skin.

Until he pounced with a growl... and she squealed.

And *laughed.*

An honest-to-God laugh that rode the high of her surprise.

Dedicated male lips went to the mark on her neck, stubble scraping delicate skin as he lavished her with unexpected, tender attention. When he nipped, and played, pressing her down into a mattress that did not reek of decades of sex. When he smiled back where no one could possibly see, a twist knotted in the bond. Right in her guts.

A belly flip.

One that fell abruptly away when the First Alpha lost his grin. "It's time for Alec's punishment."

Reality smashed her pretend world to bits.

She was going to be sick.

Moving her mouth as if words might come out, she so wanted to ask if her boy could be spared.

Had she not played house well? Did she not allow them all to screw with their new toy in whatever way they saw fit?

"A whipping." Touching his nose to hers, Caspian purred. "He can keep his hand. *This time.*"

Swallowing, she nodded as if promising there would never be *another time*.

"And you will stand before my men, and watch. At my side." Voice dropping in tone and thickening with warning, he added. "A loyal, marked Omega."

Cold, teeth rattling, Wren nodded again.

"Don't disappoint me." That final warning given, Caspian threw back the covers to show that both Kieran and Toby stood near enough to grab and pin her down. And both of them wore unyielding expressions, measured her, ready to spar.

"Come." In his hands, Toby held clothing. A

luxury they had denied her since dragging her chained from a cage. "We don't have much time."

THE DRESS WAS WHITE, bridal. Completely inappropriate for the grungy Waterworks or the disgusting crowds gathered within. Already the dragging hem had grown saturated, lace catching on old cement and sodden from the pooling water caught in uneven slabs. It clung to her figure.

A shroud that left her bitten arms bare to the cold.

Still she sweated.

Nerves gnawing at her guts, banked by a stalwart Caspian and an unsmiling Kieran, mist rained down on her head.

Damp hair began to curl into itself, to stick to her skin.

Several levels below, Toby, wielding a bullwhip, had her boy chained to a wall for all the Syndicate to see.

Crack.

She'd twitched at so loud a noise.

A tickle, he'd told her. Some blood for show.

Yet her boy was screaming, every cell in Wren shouting for her to kill all who stood between her and her child.

Crack.

So much blood. The ear-piercing screams of an innocent.

And she could not go to him… because those who had gathered had not come to this place to see a kid tortured. They had come to stare at her. The defeated Omega Caspian had bitten. The wild thing who had survived her Omega rampage and been cowed by their great leaders.

To see if she'd snap under pressure and entertain them once more with her death.

Crack.

The unbroken pinky finger of her left hand curled around the nearest living support. Wren took the hand of the man responsible for her boy's torment, held it with all she could, because she could not bear this alone.

The intimate touch before his men… Caspian allowed it.

Just as he allowed her silent tears to run free, the convenient mist concealing every trace.

Crack.

Four strikes and Alec had lost the ability to stand, hanging from chained wrists like a broken doll.

Crack.

Voice grown hoarse, the boy's screams no longer

reached her ears. Though his shoulders shook with visible sobs.

Crack.

Lavender eyes turned away from the rivulets of blood running down the flesh of her beloved child. They settled on a muddy brown gaze.

Caspian, the arrogant and deceitful king, saw everything.

Unmitigated despair.

Crack.

Squeezing the tiny finger she had hooked to his palm, he offered. "It won't kill him."

And that justified this?

"The kid came to me. He took an oath when he joined, swore to forsake all family. That was his choice."

Crack.

"Which means"—significance burned in that treacherous gaze—"that he is no longer your boy. He belongs to me."

Always. Alec would always be her boy.

Even when he was old and gray. Even after her body had long since decomposed in the mud, Alec would be her boy.

Crack.

Love, she felt pure emotion even in that horrible moment. And Wren knew Caspian could feel it churning in her. And knew that the Alpha was well aware it was not for him.

Crack.

His eyes narrowed, a less than subtle reminder that this was her punishment too. A test that, should she fail, would be the end of more than just her life.

Alec who suffered. Mikael who healed. Both were nothing to him.

Crack.

That was why she'd been paraded before his slaves, his servants, his whores, and his Syndicate. An Omega. A woman he'd defeated at her most dangerous. Who he'd mounted in abject victory. Who he had marked in a frenzy of violence that would never leave her skin.

Crack.

Each lash might as well have been lain to *her* flesh.

"That's enough!" Caspian's voice boomed across the massive space. Loud enough that even a thousand gallons of rushing water could not drown out his bark. "Punishment has been served."

Panting from the exertion of wielding the whip, Toby cut a glance over his shoulder. Then he turned, bare chest covered in a myriad of tattoos. He looked right to her.

The way her bones vibrated, Wren knew he called through their link, demanded that she give him her attention. But she couldn't. She couldn't lift her eyes away from the weight of Caspian's stare.

She would never be able to look at Toby again.

"It could have been the kid's hand. Remember that, pretty mouse, before you hold a grudge." It wasn't Caspian words that made her flinch, it was what was buried far beneath them—a hint of regret.

It was as if even a megalomaniac of his proportions had finally recognized that what he'd done had… eternal repercussions.

As if the thought had never occurred to him.

As if his unsettled feelings were foreign, uncomfortable.

What vibrated from him was too subtle to be called guilt, and too selfish to be culpability.

His concern was utterly selfish, the male bothered by the loss of something he'd never had to begin with.

As if to offer this recognized deficit that lingered between them, he spoke over her head. "Kieran, have the boy taken down and put somewhere dry."

Her face was so warm, the splints binding her fingers creaking from the force she'd exerted gripping Caspian's hand for support. Which had to be why her bones protested when she let go, her fingers slipping from Caspian's grasp.

8

———

"No."

No?

Back in Caspian's den and away from the eyes and ears of his men, Wren had wept. The ugly kind of sobs that left one rocking themselves and breathless.

Curled up in the corner, sopping wet from the waterworks downpour, her dress was no longer white.

Dingy, like the Alphas' whole fucking hive, it suited her.

Stuck to her skin, marking the floor where she'd plopped down in a puddle, it gave her a barrier to shut out the males when she buried her face in her knees.

After she'd purged, hiccupped, and hated, silence stole over her thoughts.

Everything felt fuzzy, disconnected—as if she'd floated beyond reality and watched from a distance.

Toby's hand on her shoulder, the very hand he'd used to wield the whip that had mutilated her boy, didn't so much as make her flinch. She'd hardly felt it at all.

Whatever he muttered to her, was lost.

But she was not lost.

She was more than one terrible collection of days.

More than the brand on her face or the bite shaped scars on her skin.

She was a mother.

And unlike the little ones dead and buried in the mud outside her home, Alec and Mikael still lived. Would thrive.

She had to help assure it. Do whatever it took to make it all better.

Alec needed her now. He needed her collected and capable. He'd need her smiles and purrs.

He needed her *medicine*.

Yes! Pushing from the ground, Wren ignored the crouching male at her side and ran to the murdered doctor's box. Rifling through the medications Toby had meticulously organized by day and hour, she knocked it all aside in search of the precious injection: a healing boost.

When her hands closed on the prefilled syringe, feeling rushed back. Holding it to her heart, excitement on her face, she'd turned to Caspian and shown him.

"No."

How could it be so simple to deny her child relief?

Yes.

"No."

Holding it out to him, she crossed the room and went to her knees, prepared to beg… lick his boots if that's what it took.

Radiating agitation, the brute fisted his hands into balls, and glared. He met her eyes and snarled, "I told you no."

Wren tried to unfurl his fingers, to put the syringe in his hand. But he was too strong. So she set her cheek to his thigh and held to his leg as her shoulders shook.

"Mouse, you are angering me."

There had to be some way to purchase mercy for her boy!

Clawing at his zipper, she pulled out a flaccid cock, feeding it into her mouth just like Rosie did. Tears streaking her face, she tried every trick she'd seen, and though he swelled, Caspian never got fully hard.

The shove that knocked her back onto the floor sent the syringe flying from her grip. Scrambling after it, Wren let out a cry when Kieran snapped it up in his hand. It was him she fell upon next, kneeling at his feet and holding onto his leg so that he could not kick her away.

No matter her debasement, the Second Alpha wouldn't even look at her.

Aloof, staring forward, he ignored the silent begging and louder sobs. He even ignored her screams when Toby forcibly peeled her away. Kieran just walked out of the room, dismissing her completely.

Striking out at the Third, she shoved him off and stood before the pair of offenders as if she stood a chance at seeing them ripped apart. Panting, smoothing her hair and trying to catch her breath before she fell into a dangerous mental state, she shook, coughing up old phlegm that rattled its way out of her chest.

And could not pull herself together even enough to breathe properly.

Enraged, Caspian threw her box of medicines, roaring, "What more do you want from me? Never have I spared a hand!"

Pills spilled over the aging rugs, bottles broke.

Next he lifted her breathing treatment machine over his head, smashing it against the distant wall. Metal split at the seams, internal bits destroyed.

"You take all this crap and still you cough! I have to hear you wheeze while you sleep. I feed you a fortune in engineered foods. And you want to give what I provide for you to a traitor? He knew you'd sold your body to me and came begging for a place anyway!"

She didn't care about the medicines or the machines. All she'd lived for had been those boys.

Wren growled… she hadn't meant to, but the insulting noise had slipped out all the same.

Both Alphas froze.

Nearest her, Toby reeked of something far deeper than anger. That was nothing to the wave of fury emanating from the First Alpha across the room.

"GET OUT!"

Stepping between her and the rampaging First, Toby held her behind his back. "I'll take her upstairs."

Nostrils flaring, Caspian's livid glare turned upon his Third. "Toss her back into the Warrens. Let her remember what life was like before I dragged her out of the mud."

THERE WAS no fight left in her when Toby dragged her from the waterworks. None.

He wasn't purring or sweet, but nor was he as rough as his anger signaled an infuriated Alpha should be. There were no words between them, only the singed buzz of an insubstantial link.

One that fluttered with… concern.

Nothing like the burn that twisted her guts from the male above. Even with Caspian far away and locked in his den—she could feel his tumultuous wrath. Feel how it was blended with desperate lust as he thought to slake such feelings on the body of another.

She could sense his confusion when the simple act of fucking was not enough to assuage the tempest.

And because both males and been arrogant enough to force a half-formed link on her, *they* sensed her total disgust. Her hatred. Her disappointment in their failings as men.

"You need to cool off for a few days." Toby snarled between clenched teeth, openly angry with her. "Stay out of his reach before you push him to ruin what we have."

His grip on her arm tightened, the Alpha marching her along like a child who needed to be put in the corner.

But he didn't bruise. He didn't yank.

Considering his anger, Toby was downright gentle.

He was even worried.

That did not change how he shoved her out of their building to land straight in the mud.

Knees scraped, the familiar squish of unsteady ground under her hands, Wren took in her first deep breath of outside air since she'd been taken.

It reeked of shit.

Cold air brushing naked arms, wet skirts icing in the cold, she picked herself up… and felt utterly alone.

The long walk home did nothing to ease her distress. Not when neighbors took one look at her and turned their backs.

Everyone knew who she now belonged to.

And reviled her for it.

Planks rocking under her bare feet, heart worn, she dragged her sorry bones all the way to her busted door.

No longer did she have a home. Mud had been tracked all over the floor, items cast aside and broken when looters deemed they held no value.

It was as if she'd never existed. Her life in this sorry den erased.

The scent of her boys did not even linger in the air, the smell of rot and mildew pervading each breath.

No wonder they had all been sick…

She was a terrible mother.

One of her boys lay in the hospital fighting his weak lungs for life. The other had been beaten bloody and left to hang before a gang of thugs.

And this room, this place that had been her home was so beneath what they deserved that her skin itched just standing in its walls.

So she left.

Walking around the sinking skyscraper she'd carved out a room in, she climbed over a fence made of scrap. Her skirt caught, tore, and left a lace trail that ran through soggy mud. She didn't care. Not when she was so busy hating herself for ruining her boy's chance at a better life.

Curling up in a place she had spent many of her worst hours, Wren shut her eyes and shrunk in her skin.

"He's just a kid. A stupid one, but still." It was the last person she expected to hear. Tawny hair falling in his eyes, Kieran stood over her. In his hand was an empty syringe.

Palm opening, it fell into the mud.

Turning to walk away, he snarled over his shoulder, "Tell anyone I gave it to him and you'll die for it."

9

———

*W*ait!

He hadn't seen her hands sign the entreaty, ignored her pathetic throat sounds as she fought the mud to stand.

Rushing to catch Kieran before he slipped away, Wren threw her arms around his middle and held him with all her might.

He froze, stiff as stone under her arms, but he didn't push her away. He didn't slap her face or snarl.

The Second Alpha only stood there, as if unsure what to do.

Face pressed to his broad back, Wren breathed in the familiar scent of potent male—flooded with a burst of true gratitude and unadulterated appreciation.

Had she words, so much would have tripped from her lips. Had her fingers not been splinted, and had he the knowledge to understand her sign language, she would have told him that she would never forget his kindness to her boy.

"What are you doing?" This strained voice Wren did not even recognize.

Without allowing the awkwardly motionless male out of her grasp, Wren crept from his back to his front—so he might see her face, view her wide, glistening eyes.

All the filth she'd brought with her from the ground smeared his clothing, making it look as if he almost belonged in this dump. As if they were a matched set. And she should have apologized for ruining his clean things, but there was no way she would let him walk away without letting him know how much this meant to her.

Kieran didn't seem to notice her filth, not when he stared down at her with a complicated blend of emotions playing over his face.

Confusion dominated. Under it sat annoyance. Intrigue. Disbelief. Anger.

She needed him to understand. Ear to his heart, she hugged him not only in gratitude, but because holding someone in that moment lifted such a burden.

He had given her air when she was drowning.

He had saved her from the worst kind of self-doubt.

And he had comforted her boy, even if Alec never understood what had been injected into his veins.

Wren knew Kieran desired to leave. That he hated her. She'd even take his coming beating without so much as a cry of protest so long as she could silently display how she felt.

Just for this one moment where she knew her boy had been given a secret, precious gift. Where the man who had delivered it let her take comfort in him, even though he disliked her.

She took her moment with full enthusiasm, with a smile and the purr reserved for actual happiness.

When his grip came to her horribly tangled and mud spattered hair, she didn't resist. Scalp tingling from the pressure, from the strength of his grip, she was made to lift her head.

The face looking down at her was a stranger's.

He moved so quickly she'd barely had time to draw breath. One moment she'd been hugging the villain who'd taken pity on her child, the next she was slammed against the sagging wall of her building.

By him.

Because he was kissing her as if he'd die without another taste.

Kieran, who never kissed when he fucked her.

Startled, her purr stumbled into a whimper. He swallowed it, the entirety of his body pressed against her slight frame in the dark.

The noises coming from him were desperate, the force of his body rubbing against hers imprinting the wall into her skin.

And then a second later he was off of her, panting, green eyes burning as if she had done him harm.

Chest heaving, knowing she looked utterly befuddled, Wren kept herself painted against the wall.

The male pacing before her, the one manically running his hands through tousled tawny hair, was a stranger.

You hate me.

But he glared at her with such longing.

You use me like a disposable doll.

Stopping long enough that his boots sunk a good two inches into the mud, he cut her a glance, looked about ready to rip her head from her shivering shoulders... as if he heard her silent tirade.

And then flew at her again.

Tongue and teeth and lips that gave no quarter, he didn't care that she barked out an alarmed cry.

He blocked out the sky with his mass, held her pinned so the mud could not suck her down further, and rocked his hips against her belly with manic jerks.

Wet warmth that had not come from mist or mud marked her stomach, the male spilling so much precum the outside air would waft the aroma for all those near to sniff.

A dangerous Alpha was fucking, laying claim. Do not disturb.

Caught up in his impatience, Kieran began to bunch up her tattered dress.

It was as if he didn't even realize there was more than his urges before him. One second he was growling for her slick, the next he had freed his cock and rammed it so deep inside her, Wren's teeth snapped together.

Tongue invaded her mouth, he whined and bucked and pulled at her hair.

This was not the calculating seducer who only gave her pleasure with pain, the one who degraded her and did all he could to make sure she hated him.

This was a man possessed.

A man who was arrestingly rough and infinitely gentle.

Her back would be gouged with bits of cement wall, her pussy was screaming that he was too big, that she was stretched too full.

That his looming knot would see her in tears.

Yet her bowed body reveled in it, despite the fact

that he pumped into her in the most horrible of locations.

A graveyard.

The mud that held her shame.

It was as if it didn't matter. As if she was absolved.

As if this was what it should always feel like with a male.

Before Wren might even register what twisted her toes, an orgasm of epic proportions left her screaming into the mouth of a man she didn't know at all.

His following knot was set deep, bursting out and interlocking them together in a way that left them both vulnerable.

All it would take was one thug slamming him on the back of the head with a rock. One freezing neighbor to drive a blade between their ribs to steal their clothes.

Sagging until mud squished Wren's back, the pair of them took to the ground.

He wouldn't meet her eyes, his own cast to the side as if he was in pain.

As if he felt *guilt*.

The warmth of his following burst, the twist of her vaginal cavity squishing his meat tight distracted just enough she didn't realize how deep she'd sunk into the mud.

It covered her ears, creeping up her cheeks and about to fill her mouth.

The Second Alpha, his head thrown back, sucked in a hearty breath. Tossing his gaze her way, his breath caught and he yanked her out of the mire.

Dragging her out of the mud, he climbed up the scrap heap she'd piled for her fence and kept them both clear of the very mud that was slowly devouring Dale City.

Metal digging into the fresh cuts Kieran's enthusiasm left on her back, Wren watched her breath fog in the night. Felt her delicate tissues pulsate and beg for more fluid from the fat cock inside her.

Whimpered when Kieran dumped another hot load of cream deep into her belly.

His knot expanded all the larger.

A knot the Alpha could not resist grinding deeper as he ripped open her filthy gown and lapped at her nipples.

Raw, tingling, exhausted, broken-hearted, world-weary, Wren lay back on her sharp metal scraps, eyes to the sky, while her unsplinted fingers played in tawny hair.

"Neither of those kids are your blood. Why waste the effort?"

The entirety of his voice was foreign, innocent. And, this was the first honest question Wren had ever heard from the pretentious, cocky male.

Hand to his chest, Wren pressed Kieran to sit up so that she could display the muck-filled yard he'd found her in.

Gated by debris and soppy with too much wet—where the syringe Kieran had dumped at her feet had been swallowed by mud, Wren laced her working fingers in the silent, brooding, utter fool's hand.

Even surrounded by such a place, Wren knew Kieran had no idea what his eyes fell upon. She knew he didn't see.

But she looked at him all the same, and pet his arm as if he were the lost child looking for a home.

Behind them, so many little bodies were lost in that mud. Some sinking, some rising. A sharp eye would see the bits of sun-bleached bone poking out here and there. They would see the little markers etched with names rain and wind had worn clean.

There had been little Faith, barely hours old when Wren had found her squalling in the mud. Tossed away like garbage at the Warrens' gates. Even though she'd been only a child herself, Wren had taken her home, named her something suitable for those large, wise eyes, and held her to her breast the entire four days it took the baby to die of starvation.

Because Wren had no milk and could find no one who might trade with a penniless mute.

She had *begged* at the gates that separated her sector from the higher levels.

Been kicked, ridiculed, and spit upon.

Stiff with rigor mortis, wrapped in the prettiest cloth Wren could scavenge, the poor thing was properly buried. Weighted down with debris so her little body would not float up in the mud, Wren had scooped mud over the shallow hand-dug grave.

That was only the first infant Wren had stumbled upon over her years in this hell. So many tiny babies cast off to squeal in the muck for milk she'd never be able to provide.

It was those graves she pointed at first.

Kieran looked where she directed, eyes squinted and openly restless. So she'd cradled her arms in an unmistakable position and rocked them. As if they'd held a baby. She pointed to another bubbling mound. Same motion. Again. Again. Again.

Older kids were cast off too. Gwen, Cecily, Brandon, Xerxis, Palo… on and on their names went.

Very few had lasted longer than a month.

Some she got to hold a whole year.

Only Mikael and Alec had lasted long enough to have an actual future.

The Alpha still knotted inside her looked, then glanced back when Wren signaled the height of the child who was buried. She pantomimed a terrible cough.

Beside that grave slept a boy, one who'd been older than Alec when he'd passed. Who had been strong and smart. Wren pantomimed vomiting.

Each lost little life… she told their story without a single word. Starvation, violence, disease… an accident. She made the great Kieran bear witness. She made the bastard *see* what the Warrens really was.

Hell.

To his benefit, when he had seen enough, he set his forehead to her breast and said nothing. He never asked how many bodies she'd had to weigh down with bricks so they wouldn't float to the surface. He didn't ask their names or how she'd found them.

He just listened to everything she couldn't say.

All the while his knot pulsating between them.

All the while his lips brushing over hers as if they were lovers and not the bitterest of enemies.

10

____

Dress in shambles, bodice shredded down the middle in a way Wren would never be able to mend, she broke from Kieran's hold when at long last his knot subsided. The panting male still hovered, tensing when she shuffled away—yet this was what he'd continuously demanded from her each time he fucked her in Caspian's den.

"Get off me. Others do it better."

Wren had no doubt that they did. And she'd never cared about impressing him.

She just functioned because she had a goal. Save Alec. Heal Mikael.

Survive and try not to smirk at the scars she'd set into their skin in her rampage—avoid staring at their healing noses and black eyes.

Yet in the foggy dim of the Warrens' night, it was not a sneer twisting Kieran's lips when she pulled away. It was a frown.

Shivering from the loss of his heat, a light groan accompanying the movement that rammed a jagged bit of scrap against her spine, she shifted her attention from him—from that pained expression—and took a good hard look at herself.

Caked in drying mud, more naked than clothed, warm semen slipping from her slit to instantly chill on her thighs…

And healthier than she had been in years.

Hip bones no longer jutted out. Her bared breasts had fullness and weight.

She shivered.

"You're cold." It was as if he gnawed his tongue, biting back unspoken slander. "You will go inside your home and you will not come out."

Wren shuffled back even farther, lavender eyes leaving her filthy body to take in the Alpha.

The Alpha tucking away his somehow still hard dick.

Kieran fought the teeth of his zipper before scrubbing his jaw with his palm. "Knowing Toby, he's already prepping a transport of food and water for delivery."

Doubtful. Wren could feel her bones shaking with his madness. Toby was ripping rooms apart and screaming at the sky, nowhere near the right state of mind to organize such a thing. But that didn't matter.

Trying and failing to cover her breasts with the remnants of her bodice, Wren nodded anyway.

"If I find out that you didn't heed this order, if I hear a peep about you scavenging or trying to run, I'll cut off a whole lot more than the kid's hand." This was the domineering Kieran she knew, the one whose words dripped malice. The one who stood over her and threatened. "Do you understand me, Jax?"

There was no argument. Only an idiot would scamper around the Warrens with her tits hanging free. Just smelling of Omega was a recipe for a violent death. She told him as much when she gestured toward her exposed chest and pussy.

When green eyes lit on cold pebbled nipples, drifting lower to where his seed leaked out, they came alive with more than just anger. "What does it feel like, that bond you got with them?"

Hmmmm.

Curious Kieran would have been slightly amusing had Wren not been shivering in the cold. Tired, and thirsty. Her body had grown spoiled by access to life's necessities and already complained about the lack.

Hugging herself to preserve warmth, she

gnawed at her lip and felt exactly how Caspian's and Toby's half-formed bonds worked against her.

"Well?"

No point in brushing it off, she pointed to her guts and mimed a twisting cramp. That was Caspian, who even from this distance she could feel fumbling through the pinging in his guts with women and a great deal of drink. Each climax that erupted from his cock Wren felt a ghost of sensation building at the base of her spine to burst and leave her insides completely unfulfilled.

She knew he suffered.

She knew he could not comprehend the cause.

He didn't sleep though the hour was late.

He felt the foreign pings of worry.

Lacking the ability to feel her out properly while gorging on his lustful appetites—it distracted him. Because he felt something was *missing* though he had surrounded himself with everything.

She wondered if he'd even jolted at her earlier burst of gratitude toward Kieran, or if he'd been too busying knotting his entire pen to grasp that that wondrous emotion had come from her.

Had he recognized her orgasm with his Second was not part of his physical pleasure?

Probably not.

That would require him to look past his own selfish interests and see her as more than just property. He would have to actually care to tune into the tiny two-way connection between them for more than a self-indulgent reminder of a terrible victory.

And a man like him, wasn't capable.

Next Wren ran her palm over her shoulder, her arm, pointing to joints to signify the bones underneath. This was where she felt Toby. Bone deep, resonate, the frame that held her together utterly affected by him.

Male obsession tingled in a constant state of vibration. There was also adoration, determination, and guile.

Were she not certain he raged in the Pipeworks, she wouldn't be surprised if he were standing in the shadows watching her now—watching this with a smile.

Twisted guts and endless tingles, that ebb and flow and subtle taste of other emotions. And this was not even a full bond.

To explain to Kieran his effect on her, she caught the tip of a nail against his neck, drawing it slowly down until the Alpha broke out in gooseflesh.

Openly shivering, he closed his eyes, and let his head fall back while she extended the sensation.

Purring without thought, shoulders relaxing, it seemed he begged for more attention, but her lesson was over.

She was tired.

Voice soft as it had been that first time he'd seduced her on the floor of her home, Kieran said, "Go inside. Don't come out."

No food or water arrived that night.

No clothing or a source of heat.

Lying where she'd once had a nest, ancient linoleum under her body, Wren spent the night in icy cold.

Teeth chattering, mud freezing until she might crumble it off with her hands, she faced the kind of chill that killed.

Had she been warmer, she might have sensed grievous danger.

Had her joints not been locked in stiffness, she might have made it out.

But the ground had already been shaking long before her chattering teeth realized it was not just her body that rumbled.

The home she knew was destined to sink, was already descending into a torrent of mud. It oozed through the bars on her windows, ran in a river through her buckled front door.

And buried her no matter how she flailed and fought the tide.

Sucked under, encapsulated, Wren was caught in the drift.

Her pale arms flailing in the onslaught was the last view of his mouse Caspian saw before his cameras cut out, the Alpha screaming for his men to muster and dig her out.

But it was too late.

Several floors of Wren's sinking building had been claimed by the mud before they arrived.

And she was gone.

11

————

Chest expanding, the human leather of his coat stretched and creaking with each great pant, Caspian shot daggers at the sunken shit heap. Thirty-four floors still stood, Dale City's engineers bracing the building far above the stink of the Warrens... while simultaneously doing nothing for those who had lost their homes in the mud.

Warrens rats were beneath their notice.

Just as they were beneath Caspian's.

All but one, at least.

Every inhale was laced with sharpness, every exhale burdened with an angry growl. No one neared him save Toby, who clawed at his shaved head, mattering beneath his breath as he manically paced.

The Third Alpha had already torn long gashes into his scalp, clawed his veined forearms to shreds—self-mutilation keeping him level enough to shoot his First Alpha a hateful glare.

"Twenty-four hours you said. A whole fucking day with no food or water. No blanket—punishment for being the perfect Omega who loved her brood. Had you not interfered, I would have been here with her, boss! She wouldn't have died!"

"Watch your tone." The warning had been spoken lowly, but it seemed the hundreds on the scene froze.

Toby, nostrils flaring, showed his teeth. "You murdered our mate."

The barest of flinches. Knuckles cracking, Caspian looked away from the bubbling mud for the first time since arrival and set the full weight of his displeasure upon the seething Third.

Mindlessly picking at an oozing cut, Toby narrowed his eyes. "And now she'll never know estrous. I'll never fully bond her. And you... the ghost of your marking *my sunshine* will always ping in your chest. You're half-bonded to a dead Omega. Only way to wipe her clean from your corpse is to fully bond another. And when you do, I'll see her drowned in mud."

Kieran stepped between them. "You know how

he gets, sir. Pay Toby no mind. A day or two and he'll remember his place."

There were eyes on them, eyes that would report to rival gangs. To government. To his own men. They could not show dissension. But later… Toby was a dead man. "Leave."

"Try and move me, and you'll have a show on your hands that will echo through the city for fucking years." And his Third meant every word, digging his feet into the soggy ground and bracing to be charged. "I'm not leaving until they pull her body out."

Her body…

The thought of a limp, lifeless mouse hanging from a worker's arms like a rag, stole Caspian's next breath. She'd be blue under all that mud. Stiff.

How much water would it take to wash her clean?

Odd feelings accompanied such thoughts like barbed wire corded through his belly, squeezing as it cut deep. Vomit came to Caspian's mouth, swallowed back down by an act of pure willpower.

"They won't find her, sir." Kieran crossed his arm over his chest, looking to the building. "To dig down that far… she's buried with her children. I think that's what she'd want."

Brow cocked, Caspian turned his glare to the handsome one. "What?"

Was his Second growing fucking red-faced?

"I asked you a question, Kieran."

"The kids she found." Clearing his throat, the Second pointed to a patch of mud now littered with massive debris. "The ones who died. A dozen, maybe more, are buried there."

Reeking of jealousy, Toby shoved forward. Inches from the Second, his finger kissing the trigger to the firearm hanging from his shoulder, he demanded. "She doesn't talk to you. You can't read her hand signs. How do you know that?"

"The dying kid in the hospital told me." The answer came on a hiss, a bristling Second unflinching before the manic Third.

Kieran was lying, Caspian could always tell. And had Toby been in his right mind, he too would have seen the tick that betrayed their pack-mate.

"Enough." There had been more than enough antagonism. More than enough insubordination. More than enough of that vicious feeling pulverizing his guts to a pulp. "The men keep digging."

FINGERS FIGHTING THE CLASP, the rusty thing finally gave and the cache's lid groaned open.

Reaching for a canteen of drinkable water, the top was twisted and brought to cracked lips. Swallowing all she could, Wren gagged, spit up gritty mud, and bought that rust-flavored nirvana back to her lips.

Every muscle shook, strained and aching now that panic had subsided.

The rest of her dress she'd lost swimming for the hatch. Clothed only in dirt, fucking staggering and tired and sick, she'd dragged her aching bones away from a building that might tear free of its moorings and fall.

No Warrens rat would scamper near a sinkhole. They always got worse. Those fresh fools who came to scavenge always died.

Run to higher ground.

And if they were wise, sneak to a stash.

Because those who knew this dump had lost at least one home over the years. Starting over with nothing was a death sentence.

Wren had four ancient canteens of water. She had clothing for herself and her boys.

There was even a single pricy package of rations she'd hidden away.

But this place was not safe.

Which was entirely why she'd put the small case of treasure here.

Ancient wallpaper sagged on moldy walls, flocked with growing fungus and faded by time. There was water in the pipes. Tainted water enough to wash half the mud from her unsteady frame.

There were stairs that led down into a half sunken foyer of what had once been a grand hotel. There were bodies rotting in the muck.

This was a dumping ground for the dead.

Unclean. Infested.

And also her salvation.

Pulling coarse fabric over her damp arms, Wren found warmth for the first time in hours. Choking down the precious rations, she found a belly that no longer ached.

Stuffing her face almost brought with it a feeling of guilt, but it's not like she could take food with her. She'd be murdered the instant someone thought there were edibles to be found in her pockets.

So long as the lids hung off to show they were empty, drained canteens she could hawk for supplies.

Goggles were a necessity.

Tools for salvage.

First on the agenda was finding a new home. Someplace where she could wait out her finger bones healing. Until then, there was no point in going back to the males.

She had to be able to say her piece.

Caspian owed her a years' worth of water. He owed her coin.

And by their original agreement, she'd only had to serve until he was tired of her.

Since he'd cast her off, she was pretty sure that was that.

Of course, he'd probably kill her the instant she demanded payment for whoring, but Alec and Mikael needed funds to get out of this hellhole.

Mud clogged her ears, her pinky finger gently trying to dislodge what a rinse in old pipes had only pushed deeper. That ate up the hours of her day.

That and a great deal of restless sleep.

She would get through this, just as she'd gotten through the torrents of mud looking to pin her down.

Just as she'd survived abandonment and squalor.

Just as she'd survived the Pipeworks and the Alphas who haunted them.

Two boys were counting on her. And she was going to see them safe.

12

———

Flexing under dirty bindings, Wren stretched her healing fingers, clenched them against the brace, and hissed when an ache shot down her arm.

Bones seemed ready to be free of uncomfortable splints, the bruising had almost totally faded, but muscles were weak.

And so very stiff.

A bit of old leather between her teeth, and she continued the exercise, breathing through the irritation until her fingers grew too weary to follow commands.

Then it was the next hand's turn.

Four days she'd stuck near a new, unfurnished hole. Sleeping alone for the first time in years, Wren had felt a strange liberty in the solitude.

How much simpler it was to score food when there was only one mouth to feed.

Though she was perpetually thirsty, she'd found more than enough water to keep her alive.

And the ease of it, the relief she had only one person to see through to the next day, left her in a state of deep guilt that she'd enjoyed the respite.

So she punished herself with hard labor. Despite her fear, Wren crept up to the outskirts of the Waterworks every dawn and dusk, eyes peeled for a boy who might have been cast out.

Not a single sign of Alec was found.

Nor had Mikael been thrown out into the mud.

But she could not trust Caspian to keep either of them much longer. Not when his end of their link jittered and shook.

Inebriated. Pussy drunk.

Disgusting.

Tormented.

Raw.

Just like he liked to think of her—a *raw* mouse with so much to devour.

Toby's echo in her bones wasn't much better. All she sensed from him was anger. The cunning kind that held a smile on its face and a knife at its back. Neither seemed ready to forgive her outburst. Neither had a moment's peace.

Even though it had been days.

Putting Wren in a difficult position. How was she to face them if they would not hear her? How was she to negotiate for riches that had been promised?

Left with the niggling thought that the only way to keep her boys alive was to steal them back, she debated avoiding the raging males at all costs. But if she were caught…

Spitting out the leather, Wren's teeth worked her lip as she deliberated.

Caspian was a liar of epic proportions who cared only for himself. There was a large chance he would never pay her her due.

How many times had he already gone back on his word?

But he had also marked her with myriad bites in his furious passion. Bites she would make him see when she came for her due. And if approached before his men, their First Alpha would lose face for denying his *bonded* Omega.

Such action made him look weak, and that was her greatest weapon against his damaged character.

But she *needed* a voice. She *needed* her hands so Toby might translate.

Yet they still fucking ached.

Frustrated, Wren studied the honeycombed splints, her nails only just starting to grow back.

Sitting there in the dark, flickers of the battle

stole into her thoughts. When these hands had been broken, she'd made the men roar. And if there had been only one brawny Alpha to face? He would have died.

But three, moving in tandem? Three circling and countering her swinging rebar?

Indomitable.

The memory of smashing that cement crusted pole right into Caspian's snarling face bubbled up. Smiling, Wren laid down on her side and almost felt pride.

Sheltered inside a gaping crack along the outer walls of a sinking building, little wind reached her. There she waited out the sun, hours left before she might forage safely.

Cement was still cold, but she had layers to warm fattened limbs.

Someday she might even have another nest.

But right now she had something far more important. She had purpose, and she had delicious snippets of rage-heavy memory to entertain her through the wait.

Chuckling, her teeth snapped shut. Between them was the phantom of the bite she'd taken out of Kieran's perfect ass. He'd howled, he'd snarled, and she had laughed as his blood filled her mouth.

How had she not seen that in all the matings since?

Because he always kept his back from her. He'd *hidden* it.

Which was a pity since fractured memory claimed he'd tasted divine.

Cunt clenching, Wren's cheeks went hot. Unwarranted slick swished enough to wet her pants, horrifying memory stealing in to remind the female there was so much more to that ass biting moment. Such as the huge cock that had knotted her still, Caspian's cock that she'd ridden like a veritable demon.

How could she do that?

Pressing her hands over her ears, she denied the guttural and filthy banging around in her head. Refused to acknowledge that they had come from her.

Drawing deeper into her jagged crevice, Wren shut her eyes and tried to slam the door on her thoughts.

But the mind refused to obey.

The images that played out in abandon were…

Lurid.

The smell of male. The taste of cum and sweat and blood.

The feel of pleasure in a broken body that could not feel pain.

The longing…

Worst of all, Wren had to acknowledge that

when Caspian had set his teeth to her throat, she had egged him on. And this was after her limbs were bleeding from his snapping teeth. After he had torn into her body and harmed her for his pleasure.

She had offered the Alpha an invitation. Turned up her throat for his violence.

At that moment, the steady disassociation that had kept her going through the lonely days in hiding cracked.

How could she?

How could she submit herself to the very male who had harmed her boys?

Warm, salty water wet dirty cheeks. In the distance, two Alpha males felt the shift, their ears pricked.

"SHE'S ALIVE."

13

———

Another muted gush. Cum twitched into whoever was riding his cock, but Caspian felt nothing. A sea of beautiful female bodies crawled over him, clever fingers, clever tongues, tight cunts and pretty breasts. Drowning him in carnal attention.

Yet the First Alpha couldn't even tell who was in the room.

They sucked; he stared off into space. They lapped and stroked; he called for more to smoke.

Nothing would dull the throbbing ache that had somehow moved from his guts to his chest.

He couldn't eat.

Every breath stretching his barrel chest was worse than the last. Sometimes, when the drugs hit him just right, he dreamed his lungs were filling with mud. Always he longed to hear the unwell cough that had woken him in past nights.

Missed the scent of his mouse but could not bring himself to seek her things.

He had not been back to his rooms since the mud had sucked her down, preferring the consuming distraction of his favorites in the pen. Naked, coated in female fluids, and coming down from a hideous headache, Caspian lay, daring for the first time in days to close his eyes.

Which carried him straight to the worst kind of hell. The kind where he felt his mouse's final desperation like a knife to the guts. Today it was only a dull throb of sad determination, of thirst and hunger. But as he suffered the torment, the bad feelings abated— as if a window had opened and sun streamed in. From the fragment of their link came joy, pride… arousal?

His dick twitched and someone, Caspian didn't even care to look, latched on.

The slippery tongue felt like sandpaper, the rolling wave of hands over his sack like slimy filth.

Pushing the bobbing head away, eyes still shut tight, Caspian drew in a breath of relief when his cock popped free of unwelcome lips.

Longing teased at all the internal places where he ached and rotted… *embarrassed longing*. The very feeling that plagued the mouse when he'd knotted her just right. When he held her close no matter if she was angry. A special feeling she only resonated with for him.

When she had been left to Kieran's devices, she never longed for him. Mostly she drew away from herself and survived her time with the most desired Alpha in the Pipeworks.

Her time with Toby had always left her overwhelmed and scared it was too good to be true. Yes, she longed for the Third, but the flavor was unique and pale in comparison for the few brief sips she had with Caspian.

Feeling that flutter now, knowing it wasn't the flagging drugs, aware that though his eyes were closed this was not a dream, Caspian jolted where he sprawled.

An instant later he jackknifed up. Because that distant female longing had folded into sadness, and he could practically taste the salt of her tears on his tongue.

FUCK, she's alive!

Groaning in response to rough treatment, the smooth-skinned Beta draped over his thigh wiggled in her sleep. Immediately he shoved her arms—and the touch of the other five women he'd slaked his lusts on—away. Not a single chirped in complaint when he ordered the used beauties off, not a single coy batting of their lashes or a flirty smile to tempt him back to the bed.

No, they shuffled off most likely in relief, considering how many hours he'd put them to work.

Only Rosie stood there, watching him with those big blue eyes.

Eyes that gave nothing away.

He didn't have time for her shit. Not now when his guts churned with the lightest vibration of *her*. "I told you to get out."

Pulling a pair of discarded panties from a raggedy dresser, the blonde slipped them over her hips. "Never thought I'd see you like this."

Haggard and unable to knot? Yeah, he read right between her lines. "Any of you speak of it, and I'll see you all skinned."

"Hey." Rosie held up her hands, the dispassion in her eyes matching the lack of condescending smirk he knew she was just dying to produce. "I remember what happened to Jetta."

Jetta, one of the finer pieces of leather to make up Caspian's prized coat.

Shrugging into his clothes, Caspian shot her a dark look. "What do you want, Rosie?"

"I want the big room."

"No."

She snorted a dark laugh. "Who else would you possibly give it to?"

Well the options were endless considering the stock he sheltered for his men. "Jean, Mai… that one with the curly hair."

"Naomi," Rosie offered, unflinching and unwavering. "Her name is Naomi."

That's right. Naomi who loved to eat cunt and tolerated cock.

"Please." The fact that it was a *real* please, that it was coming from so jaded a female, got Caspian to cease doing up his trousers and look at her. Once she had his eye, the Omega continued. "I want out of the pen."

Fuck no. Not with a mouth like that. His men fought over who got to spend time with Rosie. Some of them fancied themselves in love with her.

The very idea made him snort. "I don't have time to listen to you complain about how full your belly is or the temperature of your baths. So you gotta suck some cock, so what?"

"It can be like it was before, between us…" Twiddling her fingers, playing the role of sweet miss, Rosie pulled out all the stops. Just like she had when she'd caught his eye years ago. "I know what you need, what it takes to please you. I'll earn my place."

Enough! Caspian tightened his belt, dismissing her entirely. "This is about the new girl Kieran brought in."

A flash lit up the blue of her eyes. "He bleached her hair white…"

And keeps her in his rooms. A little doll made up just to look like the mouse.

Caspian had only seen the new girl once, and had almost been sick on the spot. Roaring, he'd thrown both her, and the male balls deep in her cunt, out of his pen.

Kieran was lucky his toy had gone unnoticed by Toby, or that girl would have met a bloody end.

"You fucked me almost every day the mute was here and I never complained, but this? She's been here a week and he's letting her nest, trying to breed her! Kieran promised me an out. If I can't have a baby, then at least give me the damn room!"

"Rosie." He wanted to make this crystal fucking clear. "You weren't brought here to nest. You were brought here to fuck."

Tossing her hair, she sneered. "And the big room goes to the favored whore. Who fucks better than me?"

One raw little girl did. A sweet, quiet beauty of an Omega mouse. "The answer is no."

Rosie had always had a mouth, but she had never been openly spiteful. That's the only thing that kept him from killing her when she hissed, "You fucked me the night you threw her out. You were fucking me when the ground shook, watching her on those monitors. I'm glad I got to see the look on your face when your precious mouse died."

At that, he offered the nastiest smile that might stretch apart his haggard face. "She ain't dead."

Real, the first real flicker of honest emotion betrayed the beautiful blonde. She looked repentant, maybe even worried… for the girl. "But all that mud… why hasn't she come back? If she made it out, why hasn't she come back?"

Good fucking question, but not one he was going to entertain with Rosie.

"You don't deserve her."

That didn't make any difference to Caspian. The sleek mouse was his. And she was alive.

The door banged open, a panting Toby rushing in to shout, "Boss—"

He knew, he felt her too. "Call the men. We'll scour the Warrens and flush out the mouse. Whoever brings her back undamaged"—mud-brown eyes turned to the eavesdropping Omega who'd dared insult him, Caspian sneering—"can have Rosie for keeps."

The woman's face went white. "No!"

Before she might beg or cry, before she might cling to his leg and prattle on about her worth as an Omega, Caspian marched out the door.

Turning his back on the pen, he went to his

rooms, his eyes lingering on the pristine nest his Omega had built.

Had enjoyed.

Had even, briefly, shared with him.

And then he went to scrub days' of sour sweat and desperate unfulfilling couplings from his skin.

14

———

Holding out her last dented canteen for trade, Wren grunted at the peddler. Covered from head to toe, goggles protecting her eyes, she gestured freshly unbound fingers at the expired supplement bars.

She then held up four to signify what she desired. Four credit chips and a taste of food.

Wind whistling through the buildings, she couldn't hear the man's reply. But if he was of the mind he'd be trading her for less, she'd take the damn canteen somewhere else.

Not that she'd seen other peddlers about…

Everyone was on edge in the Warrens, but that was nothing new. Her old building tilted no matter the supports tethering it to the more sturdy structures. Like the rats Caspian liked to call them, everyone scampered about, prepared to duck the fall. And it was a fair reason to fear. When decrepit buildings finally went down, the tidal wave of destruction that followed killed off more than a few.

Though even destruction of that magnitude was not nearly as deadly as poisoned water, starvation, and everyday violence that plagued this part of the city.

When she shook her head at the offer of three chips instead of four, it seemed the huffing trader was willing to make the barter. Credits and a single bar of food were placed in her hand, and he smiled, decaying teeth on display. Canteen offered, not so much as a word spoken between them, Wren took what might buy her three days of sustenance and began to turn.

The wind died down just enough for her to hear him say, "…I'll share the bounty, scavenger."

Whatever he was talking about, she didn't care. Itching her marked cheek under a faded bandana that kept her mouth free of flies, Wren left the old peddler to his table.

She had a schedule to keep. First her twilight scan for Alec and Mikael.

Slip past their favorite haunts just in case they'd been released and found their home long gone. Then, once it was dark, to the Pipeworks to see if they'd been thrown out and left in the mud.

She'd conduct the same search at dawn, and had for days.

No sign of either boy had been found. Considering that Caspian wore a coat made out of people, that he'd had a child whipped, she knew anything he did with either of them would be theatrical.

So… at least thus far… it seemed he'd done nothing.

Except cast her out, practically naked, into the mud.

Crushing down feelings of betrayal, Wren refused to acknowledge them. One could only be betrayed if one cared. She didn't. She wouldn't no matter how her eyes stung or how it sometimes grew hard to breathe.

Those Alphas didn't cherish her; they just enjoyed the novelty of fucking their very own freak. Even Toby—who wanted to take her out and rub the city's face in his defective, tattooed *mate*—thought only to parade her around, smiling that creepy unhinged grin while others scattered at the sight of them.

She was no one's mate.

This she had told herself, over and over earlier that day when she'd picked the honeycombed splints from her hand. She was her own person.

And the reminder, coupled with free wiggling fingers, left her feeling more herself than she had since waking up in a dark closet, bloody and draped with chains.

She was healthier than ever. And yes she was hungry. And *yes* she was extremely thirsty. But she could last years like this.

And she had not had to whore herself *once* since she'd fought through the torrents of mud and climbed free of her sinking building.

She had slept alone on her terms.

And as she had done before Caspian had ruined her already hard life, she had survived.

In the worst part of this city, clothes muddy and wind biting, Wren remembered pride.

And felt her heart warm—held onto that beautiful sensation, slamming the door shut on whatever ugliness the males on the other end of their links reveled in.

She was strong.

Though her fingers were weak and not every bone had healed perfectly straight, she could move them. Had practiced for hours with gentle sweeping motion and cautious stretches.

She had her *voice* back.

And now it was time.

This wasn't ideal, certainly not what she desired. But after days of deliberation, Wren had come up with no plausible alternate strategy.

In the dark of night, she had searched out potential places to make a new home. So far, nothing had been safer than the crack in the wall where she squatted. But that was no home, and there was hardly room for her body in there, let alone two growing boys. Tempted as she was to just sneak in and steal Alec, where would she take him for shelter?

There was no new home.

Despite years of trying, together they *might* find a way to climb over the gates and search out Mikael. But Wren had no idea which building housed her sick boy. And there were so many.

Tens of millions lived in Dale City.

Three credits left to her name. No food. No water. She could not provide for them like this.

She'd *need* money to buy her way out of the Warrens.

A year's worth of water could be traded for a lot, maybe even tickets out of this horrible city so they might find a fresh start.

The very thought warmed her heart further. She'd heard there were parts of the world that were still green. Distant places far beyond what even a year's worth of water and pockets full of coin might take her to.

Of course, she'd die before she saw such a place, but all she needed was a new city that would take in two boys and give them a real future. Far, far, far away from Caspian's Syndicate.

From the Alpha in his hideous coat. From brown eyes and secret smiles when no one else could see.

...she'd dreamed of him last night—dreamed of Caspian. And in the dream, he'd been kind. He didn't stink of other women. He didn't lie.

There wasn't pain or battles or mockery.

The nightmare had been horrific. The following ping in her heart when she'd awakened more than enough to make her ill.

Ripping the wrapper from her last meal, Wren shoved it under the bandana keeping the reek of shit from her nose, and fought the dry thing for a bite.

And felt...

She felt a rippling sensation wiggle and squirm in her belly. She felt a come-hither buzz in her chest.

The quasi-bond sang to her that Caspian wasn't fucking his women. He wasn't drunk or high. But he was angry, frustrated. Had been for two days straight.

Taking the final bite of her dry supplement bar, Wren swallowed a jagged bit of food down her throat. It scoured her gullet all the way to her belly.

And that was that.

To face him starving and even thirstier would make her look weak.

The splints were off, her bones had healed, she

could communicate at long last… and it had to be today.

Today she demanded her due.

He'd probably kill her.

And that… was better than living without her boys.

15

"Sir, there is an intruder wading through Pitchfork Canal 7."

For a moment, a painful beat of time, Caspian's heart stopped. Hanging his head, it took three full seconds before he found the ability to draw breath. And it shook, damn the mouse, it shook rattling its way into his lungs.

That was *her* pipe. The way she had first breached his kingdom all those weeks ago.

Unable to look at the guard who'd delivered such news, he kept his eyes on the data relay before him, and asked. "Does the intruder look small, like a child?"

"Yes, sir."

"It's her!" Toby shot around the table laden with the evil works of evil men, prepared to make a manic run down several floors of rickety rusty steps.

"We don't know that!" Caspian snarled, grabbing his Third's shoulder as he passed. But who the fuck else could it be in *that* pipe? "And if it is her, charging down there will scare her off."

They both could sense her caution, the flutters of distress and anxiety. And it was that, Caspian suspected which really stayed Toby's hand. Not his leader's order to cease.

Things between them had been… tense.

Crossing bulging arms over his chest, as if unsure what to do with the twitching limbs, Toby said, "She has no reason to run from *me*."

The Third believed it. Deep down, Toby believed there was no reason in the world the mouse might fear the Syndicate's infamous killer. And for that, Caspian had a dash of pity for the male. "We wait. If she's come for the boy, she will be captured. We'll deal with her afterward, calmly."

But continuing reports made it clear the mouse was not slinking into shadows heading the direction where the males' denned. Instead, she was climbing up the stairs, trying to blend in with the slaves.

Heading to him.

"Kieran should be told," Toby said, eyes darting left and right as if he might see her through the concrete and spy her approach.

"No." This moment wasn't for the Second. Let him stay locked in his room fucking his new toy, as he had for the last several days. The last thing Caspian wanted right now was the vitriol that bastard spewed burning the mouse's ears.

Toby didn't demand an explanation, he just backed away, as if the stairs leading from their perch were too much of a temptation to bear. Breathing hard from the corner, he snarled at the guards, "Leave."

When the trio turned toward the stairs, the Third hissed, "Not that way, you idiots!"

There was no other way for them to go. The upper levels at their backs were prohibited. And when the guards seemed confused Toby, in his infinite patience, threatened to behead their mothers if they didn't walk up, take a right, follow the hall for a hundred paces, and die there of starvation.

Without so much as a look at the madman, and his very real threats, all three obeyed.

Leaving Caspian and Toby alone on the landing overlooking the Pipeworks, waiting for the mouse.

Walking to the railing, Caspian palmed bowed metal, and peered down into the deluge. She was there, just as he had seen her that first time. And she was trying her damnedest not to turn her face up to collect some of that precious water on her tongue.

His mouse was thirsty, but would not drink his water.

She was dirty, but had not come to him to bathe.

No doubt she was also starving…

As if she felt the weight of his stare, she glanced up. But when their eyes met, even from the great distance she still needed to climb, she didn't look desperate or pleading.

She looked resolved.

No smile for him. No wave.

From their link, Caspian felt a wash of determination.

Head turning down, she gripped ancient railings and continued the climb.

"You let me think you were dead," Caspian said to no one.

It took every ounce of self-control he possessed not to run down those stairs and demand answers. Gripping the railing so hard it whined in protest, he made himself wait. Refused to show weakness before his men.

And then she was there.

Winded from the climb, she pushed back her hood and let all that glorious, mud-caked white hair fall free.

It had not been brushed, most likely in days. It was not braided and wound about her skull like the first time they'd met. It was just caught into some kind of thong, an afterthought. A burden.

Hands that would have been snow white if not for the dirt, raised before her. Squaring her shoulders, the little mouse sucked in a breath, and began.

Caspian had never taken the time to learn how to speak to her, and in that moment fucking hated that he had no clue what she said. So he blurted, "Where have you been?"

Had his voice sounded choked, unsure?

Toby, eyes unblinking, marched closer.

And she, she almost flinched.

"He asked you a question, sunshine. Where have you been?"

The confusion on her face was unmistakable. Looking between them, she signed, Toby translating, *The Warrens.*

The non-answer set his blood to boiling, Caspian barking, "Why not walk through the front gates? Why sneak in?"

Fingers moving slowly to spell out her meaning —the action obviously uncomfortable—she signed, *There are guards at the door. I knew they wouldn't let me in.*

Bloodless fists released the railing, Caspian turning to face her full on. And God, seeing her in such a state outright gutted him. "There is a bounty worth a fucking mint on your head. The

Syndicate has been combing the Warrens for days!"

So, you're going to kill me. Instantly deflated, she sagged. A despondent pretty lavender gaze slipped from him to find the floor. *I had hoped... Never mind. Just do it. Get it over with.*

Before her eyes might grow any redder, they darted back up to Caspian's, one last request on her unmoving lips. *Please don't hurt my boys.*

"Goddamn it, Caspian! I can't hear her say this shit!" Toby bellowed, "Tell her that you fucking love her already!"

Men like him didn't love, that was for the weak and the mental. Toby, for example. But that did not stop the merciless twisting dagger in his chest when she snorted at the very thought.

Sobered, she fisted and unfisted clearly aching fingers, then flourished them in her special language. But Toby did not translate.

Hissing at Toby over his shoulder, Caspian demanded an explanation. "What did she say?"

Growling under his breath, Toby snarled, "You don't want to know, boss."

"THE FUCK I DON'T!"

The little mouse jumped, loudly swallowed, and moved in the same pattern. Repeating herself.

Toby took a step closer. "It's not what you think, sunshine. He didn't mean it."

The look on her face was the most blatant kind of incredulous, the kind of look that couldn't be faked. Fingers flying she dashed out a fountain of meaning, all of it directed at Toby, who tried to follow and failed.

"You're going too fast, I can't—"

That didn't stop her. Marching right up to them, her lip curled, throat growling through the slapping violence of her unspoken words.

"Tell me what she's saying," Caspian barked, causing both a frazzled Toby and the furious mouse to startle.

"I can't fucking tell you what she's saying," Toby, hissed. "She's talking too fast!"

With an animal growl, the mouse shoved past and went to their table. Taking up paper and pen, she wrote down, and violently underlined, exactly what she wanted to say. A second later it was held right up to Caspian's face.

You owe me a years' worth of water and pockets full of credits!

"After the ground shook, I went to your house. My men have been digging ever since."

The paper slipped from suddenly slack fingers, the mouse's expression transforming from determination to disquiet.

Toby, the madman and the killer, shook his head and translated her stupefied signs.

Why would you go there? Horror was there all over her face, as if the very thought was the reason her breath hitched. *Are you crazy? You could have been killed! Don't you know how dangerous that was?*

Voice almost gentle, Caspian asked, "Is that why you left?"

You shouldn't have gone there! It wasn't safe!

"I thought you were dead..."

The pain in his voice, the fact he'd actually allowed even a modicum of vulnerability in, she flat out ignored. Her eyes went to the fallen paper.

As she stared down, so much crossed her face, the mouse never having been skilled at concealing a single thought. More so, Caspian could feel the myriad troubles that weighed her down.

A deep sense of betrayal.

The total lack of hope.

Her disgust with *him*.

So much sadness.

All he could manage to say was, "Are you hungry? Do you want water?"

Lavender eyes shot up, aflame with indignation.

"We're not going to let you leave," Toby murmured, easing ever closer. "No one is going to hurt you either."

Bending down she picked up her paper, ignoring Toby entirely and held it up to Caspian's face.

Just like the letters she'd handed him weeks ago, he snatched the paper from her fingers, tore it, and tossed it over the edge.

The bits fluttered down, some sticking to concrete walkways, some drowning in the rushing river.

The look on her face…

It didn't so much as alter when Caspian collared her neck with his grip. There was so much he wanted to say, days' worth of sick feeling that lanced him internally even now, even feeling her soft throat under his fingers.

Unrelenting in her demand, she stood under the intimidation of his scowl—not so much as flinching when a roughened palm slipped from cupping her throat to caressing her nape.

Unaware when his second hand had come to play in the mud-packed strands of her hair, when he held them to his nose for a sniff, Caspian groaned.

It was the sound of despair.

"I'll pay whatever you want if you stay. Right now. I'll fill up your pockets and give you more water than you'd drink in a lifetime. But you are not allowed to leave again. Ever."

16

———

The rich overbearing Alpha scent called to his marked female, cutting through the mud crusting up her nose and the Warrens' stink she'd dragged in with her.

With Caspian pressed so close, Wren staggered and took a graceless step back.

Countering, the First dared one of his dark smirks. "Do you agree to my terms, pretty mouse?"

Why was his voice so soft?

He wasn't even purring. There was no real word for the growl-born rattle that came from the massive male's chest. But the vibration did her in all the same.

Male fingers continued to slip over her neck and face, Caspian seeming to marvel at her filthy skin, stroking all the places it peeked from her clothing.

His pleasure in the moment churned in *her* belly, ran shivering through Wren's viscera to meld with the same enticement Toby chimed within her bones.

"Make this easy on yourself. Say yes."

Wide eyes blinking in shock, Wren didn't know how to answer.

Caspian was going to pay his debt.

She never truly expected it, yet… victory felt unexpectedly hollow.

Wrapping her arms around her middle, Wren truly felt like a prostitute.

The transaction was almost complete.

Payment for her to fuck him and his friends, so that someday she would be the one leaving his rooms to see a new, shiny girl brought in to replace her.

And that thought stirred a soul deep ache.

It had to have been written on her face, the eventual loss. The knowing that servicing men would be *forever*, as he had said.

Hand to Caspian's chest, she shifted back far enough to say what needed to be said before she made herself less than nothing.

You threw me out into the mud.

Unshakable, a liar through and through, Toby pressed his way nearer. "She says she never wanted to leave."

Wren threw the grinning Toby a sullen glare, the

Third subtly shook his head where Caspian might not see.

She tried again. *You took my boys from me.*

"The money isn't for her. It's for the kids," Toby said, twisting her words to fit a very different narrative.

Wren shut her eyes, pinching the bridge of her nose. God, her fingers hurt and it was growing hard to sign.

Why was she even wasting the effort at this point? He said he'd give her what she wanted.

After a stuttering huff, Wren got down to the heart of her real fear. *You, Toby, and Kieran made me whore.*

That particular phrase Toby seemed to have trouble translating.

I don't want to do that anymore. I kept our bargain. I did unspeakable things. Now you keep yours and you pay me what you owe.

Mud brown eyes held hers. "Why is she crying? What is she saying?"

With a pained look twitching over his face, Toby pushed his way close enough to stop her fingers. His hold unyielding, she struggled, Wren releasing a defeated whimper, as she shook her head no.

Anger growing before the word burst from his mouth, Caspian snarled. "No?"

"She says," a look of outright sedition on his

face, Toby offered, "she hated sharing you with the pen."

There was no way to counter these lies, even if they were bursting with half-truths, leaving Wren to wilt when Caspian forcibly pulled her to his chest and set his nose to her hair.

No comment was made one way or the other. Caspian offered no assurance.

He just forced up her chin and laid a brutal kiss to her lips.

Toby at her back, cutting off any chance to push away and escape, Caspian grinding a boiling-hot erection to her front, Wren was caught.

The First devoured, pawed, starved groans rushing from his mouth to fill hers.

"Please," Toby whispered at her ear, fighting her filthy clothing to expose bare skin. "Please, sunshine."

It was he, the obsessed Third who found his way into her pants first. His fingers that brushed her clit.

Bucking to escape, to seek more, Wren let out a moan that set Caspian roaring.

In tandem they tore away the remainder of her filthy things, no care for who saw, until Wren was bare before anyone who might dare look to their masters' terrace.

Both growled, but she was too thirsty to produce

more than a single gush of slick. Both licked and lavished.

But it was Caspian who spun her about, who bent her in half over his table and shoved his cock balls deep before she might fully spread.

That one manic thrust, and Caspian's knot burst forward to trap her kicking and heaving over his papers.

Back arched, Wren keened, unsure how she got there or why it felt like her insides were on the verge of explosion.

A forced orgasm drew a raw scream that echoed despite the rushing water and slaves laboring below.

Alpha cum flooded her belly, churning with the rolling rock of male hips grinding forcefully against her buttocks.

Jerking and gasping every few minutes, Caspian peppered the back of her neck with lingering kisses. It seemed more than once he tried to speak; only choked gibberish met her ears.

And all the while Toby crouched next to her and held her eyes.

The lying maniac said it, as if it made this all okay. As if he'd make it up to her. "I love you."

Pinned for ages, cunt quivering, grasping and sucking Caspian deeper each time his still hard cock spurt a fresh batch of seed, Wren saw him arrive.

Kieran, eyes sunken and face drawn, had made his way down to join his brothers.

Green eyes running over her pinned form, he looked as if he'd seen a ghost.

And indeed there was a ghost standing beside him—a pale female with long, white hair. A female who held Kieran's hand and glared with disgust at the filthy Omega speared on the table.

A near carbon copy of Wren.

"I thought I was your new little girl."

17

––––––––

Soft, reverent.

A kiss was pressed to the sensitive skin behind the spent mouse's earlobe. And though he was rarely delicate, another followed the juncture of her jawline and neck. Caspian's lips raking down the line of her throat until he set his teeth over the most vicious of his claiming marks. Biting down, a full body shudder left him loudly purring. The First Alpha relived the pinnacle of his victory over his captive Omega, teeth punched forward until his panting prize went stiff.

Slender neck in his mouth, the scent of familiar female, of her cum-laced slick, and just a soupçon of blood.

It was splendid.

So was her tiny taste of pain.

She should not have hidden herself in the Warrens. She should not have dared to deny him what was his.

But she trembled even in her pleasure. She starved. She thirsted.

She stank of equal parts shock, desire, anxiety, and resolve.

Teeth digging again into his claiming mark, Caspian could feel more than the distant flicker of her emotions—he could also feel her sudden swamp-thick mortification.

"I thought I was your new little girl."

Eyes lifting, mud-brown irises slid over what had set the female into such a state.

Kieran.

Kieran and his doll.

The new female dared a territorial whine. An Omega call for attention.

Time and time again, Caspian had seen this scene play out. *New little girls* held the foolish belief upon joining the ranks that their novelty held power. They hissed and scratched until a few months in the pen broke such undesirable behavior. Or made them more cunning.

Blue eyes narrowed in animosity, curled lip—the doll with her bleached-white hair and soft pink dress was a long way from cunning.

With a snarl, Kieran turned on the female glued

to his side, the one he had been fucking for the past week. "You were ordered never to speak!"

Bought and paid for, the Omega should have known better than to argue. "But…"

The little female with wet eyes and aghast expression, the one who stumbled when Kieran shoved her in warning, turned her attention back to Caspian's mouse.

At the female Kieran had made her up to mimic.

And fat tears fell.

They were nothing like the tracks on the mouse's dirty cheeks. Despite the forward thrust of her lip and the jumping of feminine shoulders, the act smacked of disingenuity. Not even Rosie pulled that move.

Fake tears were the work of less domesticated whores.

And the interloper's antics were clearly upsetting his mouse.

Nameless aggravation buzzed under Caspian's skin. It mutilated the bliss of knotting the mewling Omega, and stole away a portion of his triumph.

Purr pouring over his mouse, the one that had let her know that he might be savage, but that he would not hurt her, warped into a deadly growl.

Theatrics cut short on a sniff, the doll dropped her eyes to the ground and wisely took several steps back.

Intruding female silenced, Caspian's attention returned to filling the hungry cunt wrapping his cock. Rocking his hips, distracting the pretty mouse from her cringing embarrassment, it didn't take long before she lowered her lashes.

Such good behavior altered the First's vicious growl into something almost tender.

After a pathetic cringe, the Omega's internal muscles clenched, squeezing Caspian's aching cock. Grinding his knot in a twist of muscle, the female's greedy pussy managed to suck his balls bone dry, syphoning out one last, lingering spurt.

Pinpricks of pleasure gathered in the Alpha's drained sack. Sensations merged like crashing waves that broke in an erratic throb, pumping his engorged knot to a greater mass—cock kicking, eyelids drooping.

The extended groan that spilled like honey, rattled loudly—a week's worth of pent up sexual tension draining right out of his dick. Pulsating in the rhythm of his pounding heartbeat, Caspian's knot held fast, even though his body would need time to prepare fresh sperm.

This knot, this fuck, was about so much more than cum. It was about domination.

About punishment with forced pleasure.

Ownership.

Need.

He *needed* to keep her pinned to that table no matter how much her little legs kicked, no matter her grunts and frustrated sighs… no matter unwanted intrusions. No matter her shame to have another female glare at the sad picture she made.

He would keep the mouse knotted until she knew what she was.

His.

Fuck credits and a year's worth of water. That's not what she needed. Caspian would drown her in enough of him that water would be nothing. And money? He'd get her body addicted to the only currency that mattered between Alpha and Omega. And if she ever tried to hide from him for a week again, he'd have her chained to his goddamn bed. He'd fuck her until she forgot her name.

He'd revel in Toby working her ass, in Kieran shoving his dick between her parted lips.

She'd know nothing but pleasure until she purred incessantly. Until she clamped those lavender eyes on him and gave him the attention she'd dare denied hiding herself away.

He would make her need him.

"Who brought her in?" Kieran lacked the deference this moment deserved, the Second's voice growing dangerously loud. "What bastard had her all this time? Why was I not told?"

Unfurling from his crouch, no longer eye level

with the heaving mouse, Toby put his body between the Omega and Kieran's doll. "No one had her. My sunshine survived on her own."

Rage, so unlike Kieran's standard cynicism, left the Second red-faced. "She hid from us?"

The abrupt shake of his head, the elegance of his accent, Toby laid it on thick. "She didn't know Caspian placed the bounty. She snuck in thinking the guards at the gate would throw her back into the mud."

Mask of indifference snapping into place, only the tick of Kieran's cheek betrayed his undiluted anger. And in that moment, it was directed at the Alpha blocking his view of the little female bent over the table. "For you?"

Caspian didn't need to see Toby's face to know a sly smirk twisted his lips. "I *am* her mate."

Hackles rising, a vein on Kieran's neck began to throb. "The same mate who threw her out the door with no credits, no clothing, and left her to rot in the Warrens. Spare me, Toby."

Finger rising, Toby pointed right at the doll and ignored the slander in place of spitting insults of his own. "Just what the fuck is that? Some kind of joke? You dressed that slut up to look like my mate!"

"She was a gift for Caspian."

Rolling back his shoulders, limbs going loose, Toby grew ready to do more than verbally spar. "A *gift* that you happened to hide away and fuck for a week straight?"

Kieran, in a rare rage, shouted, "You didn't go to her that night. *I'm* the only one who went. *I* found Jax's house ransacked, her things gone. She didn't even have a working door."

That stopped Toby short. "Then why did you leave her there?"

"The same reason you did!"

Jaw unhinging, Caspian pulled his bloody teeth from the mouse's neck and bellowed, "Enough!"

Second and Third both turned battle-ready eyes his direction, and both dropped their gaze to where Caspian's knot no longer plugged the world's sweetest cunt. Fluids flooded between his body and hers, soaking his trousers, seeping down her trembling thighs to splatter the floor. Filthy, the mouse stank, but rinsed with his sperm, her cunt was fucking pristine. Packed full of Alpha cum, of his softening cock, of her sweet, delicious slick.

Mesmerized, as if the entirety of the argument with Toby had never taken place, Kieran muttered, "I'm next."

Subdued, but far from tame, the mouse dared to wriggle as if she had a right to get up.

Caspian returned his teeth to her throat, bit down just a touch harder, and harder yet, until the woman whimpered.

There were few things more beautiful than the sounds his silent mouse could make: The screams of defeated enemies. The constant rush of water he controlled.

Tongue raking the skin pinched between his teeth, Caspian changed his mind. Her answering nervous purr was more beautiful.

Wise of the female to appease him considering his mood.

He wanted her docile, accepting like the good little mouse she was.

Kieran dared announce his claim louder. "I'm next, Caspian."

"No!" The doll again. She rushed forward and hung on Kieran's arm, the sobs choking her voice authentic when she brushed the material on her shoulder aside to show a fresh bite mark. "You mated me."

And as if the air was not already crackling with tension, Toby began to cackle. Louder and louder it grew, maniacal and nasty, until the male was wiping tears from his eyes. "You fucking bit her?"

More laughter.

Grinding his molars, Kieran brushed the clinging woman off and snarled. "I'm Second. I fuck Jax next."

"This... this, Kieran, is fucking priceless." Toby

clapped his hands, cackling. "Let me guess; you bred her. Is that little doppelganger pregnant?"

Hand falling protectively over her belly, the toy's eyes went wide.

As if it were nothing, Kieran brushed the idea off. "She wasn't in estrous. Just high."

The girl, voice thin with disbelief, muttered, "I wasn't in estrous?"

Rounding on the female, Kieran grabbed her by the stuff of her dress. "Didn't I tell you never to speak?"

"It… it wasn't real?"

"Christ." Kieran bellowed over the railing. "GUARDS!"

Weapons drawn, three of Caspian's favored Alphas ran up the stairs. The gaping doll was cast into their arms, Kieran shouting to take the damn female and toss her in the pen.

Under Caspian, the mouse began to bang her hands upon the table, the struggles tearing her soft skin on the First Alpha's teeth.

It was Toby who put a hand on her head, who warned as gently as a killer might, "Be still."

Reluctantly, stinking of anger, she obeyed.

Caspian nuzzled her matted hair, relieved the distraction paled with the fading shrieks of the doll.

Cock slipping from her saturated channel, Caspian flipped the waif on her back, collared her bleeding throat with his hand, and leaned down close. Ignoring the aggravating males, meeting the mouse's eyes and making sure she understood every fucking word, he said, "Next time I lose my temper, I forbid you from returning to the Warrens. You'll go to the big room and you'll lock the door."

That flicker of defiance glowed like an ember in lavender eyes he'd mourned. Those lovely eyes said what her lack of voice, what her manner, never would. *That he had been the one to cast her out in the first place.*

That all they had suffered over the last week was at his hand.

And that they would never speak of it.

Caspian sealed their unspoken pact with a lingering kiss, draped over her naked, filthy body. And then he gave her a gift.

He whispered a truth at her ear. "I missed you, pretty mouse."

18

———

How could something cause pain yet still feel like home?

Caspian's warm breath fanning her cheek, Wren's pelvis free of a knot her body had not been quite ready to handle, she shivered, gnawing hunger eating her belly.

Yet did not feel misery as she should.

Perhaps it was the Alpha purr he poured upon her flesh. Maybe it was the smell of familiar male. That had to be what drew her nose to his vulnerable throat. Not that she sought comfort from this man. Not that she longed to be held properly.

Deep breaths, instinct drove her to find solace in his scent, to saturate her cells in it, to forget the stink of the Warrens and the aches in her bones.

If he'd offered her water in that moment, she

would have lapped it out of his palms like a dog. Food of any sort, she'd swallow past a gritty throat to fill an aching belly—so long as he'd been the one to place it in her mouth.

Even here. Even on display.

Having not shaved since last she'd seen him, Caspian's cheek bristled with the early growth of a beard. It scratched at her skin when she'd thrown an arm around his neck, rubbing her cheek to his in search of more scent.

Familiar, warm, steady, and powerful.

Guts churning, her skin buzzed as if she'd been drugged.

Or was that the fading remnants of panic, all of it washing away the more lightheaded she grew?

Had it not been for the hand poorly finger-combing her hair, for the little zings of pain each time a knot caught, Wren would have fallen asleep as she was.

Naked. Splayed on a work table where any with a view of their Alpha's terrace might see. Clinging to a monster.

Filthy and caged by the arms of a dangerous man.

God, she was thirsty.

Licking at her own drying tears in an effort to soothe her parched throat, a pink tongue darted, traced, and came back tasting of salt and dirt.

Hooded, mud-colored eyes took in the way she worked to swallow, and the entirety of Caspian's demeanor shifted.

The rare softening of his expression cinched crudely into the hard countenance of a leader. A remorseless killer. Eyes glazed, he reached between their bodies and cupped what still spilled from her womb, lifting the slippery pearlescent fluid and bringing it to her lips.

The offering was less about domination and more about Alpha impulse, not that it mattered. Wren swallowed what slid from his palm to her mouth.

She sucked his fingers as if she might find another drop.

Exhausted.

Shaken.

Starving for so much more than food.

A lovely, soft enticement of noise—so unlike any offering he'd made before—preceded another sip of slick-laced cum. Feeding her more of their shared fluids, Caspian held her eyes.

The male didn't blink.

"Don't interrupt them."

It sounded distant, that voice. As did the small scuffle preceding, "Get your hands off me, Toby."

"My mate needs water, food, a bath before she can handle more."

"Caspian!" The Second's call was dripping with anger.

At the sound of his name, brown eyes that had mesmerized her into a slack, purring mass snapped out of their trance. Slicing his attention to the side, Caspian said nothing.

He didn't need to. The threat of his gaze was more than enough.

Fearless in his approach, Kieran shook off Toby's grip. Chillingly cold, he staked his claim. "As Second, she's mine now. Toby has no right to fuck her, feed her, or even look at her until I give the nod."

Lips pulled back from gnashing teeth, Toby snarled like a wolf. "Watch yourself. She's my mate! Claimed!" Snapping from angry to manic, a nasty laugh cracked through the air. "You have your own now. Go play with her."

The meanness of his grin stole any beauty from Kieran's face. "You made the deal, Toby. This female is for the pack until Caspian doesn't want her. You agreed to third rank so long as you are allowed to keep her when that day comes. Until then, back the fuck off or forfeit the Warren's rat totally."

At the slander, Wren found the strength to turn her head.

Toby stared down at her with something so honest, it seemed unnatural. Adoration, a brief flash of victory, all wiped from his gaze when his eyes left her face to land on Caspian. "Boss, she can't have eaten in days. She needs water or she won't make slick. If he fucks her now, Kieran will damage her."

Warmth disappeared, the pleasing weight of male leaving her ridiculous, draped on the table like tossed aside leavings. With him gone, a modicum of dignity returned.

Rising to her elbows, legs noodly and vision swimming, Wren tried and failed to get up.

The slip and subsequent *oomph* that followed when her head banged back against the tabletop was not missed by any of the males.

Males who stared, each intense in their own way.

Kieran broke the silence. "I'm not the one who damages females, sir. Nothing I might do would kill her."

Throat working, a vein in his temple pounding out a fast rhythm, Caspian turned his back on her. And it looked as if he staggered. Tucking away his flaccid cock, the First Alpha snarled, "If I find a single fresh bruise, or the mouse is returned to me in any state other than pristine, Kieran, I'll hold you down while Toby fucks you with his mangled knot in any sick way the bastard can dream up. I doubt you'd survive it."

As if to test his First Alpha's resolve, Kieran made a grab for the reeling Omega. Female swept up over his shoulder, ass up, her leaking pussy exposed for anyone he might walk past, he brushed by the pair and carried her away.

Long past mortification or any kind of rational sense, Wren closed her eyes to it all, oblivious if a single soul saw her shame—yet painfully aware that such a display was not unusual in Caspian's Pipeworks.

19

Had the walls not been solid concrete, they would have trembled from the force of Kieran slamming the door. Despite her full-body jolt, Wren saw nothing of this—her nose to the Second's back, weak arms hanging limp.

Conserving her strength, she didn't even raise her head.

After all, there was no need to view the room to know where they were. The musk of old and new sex permeated the air, cloying and tart... telling.

The big room.

And it reeked of fresh and clotted fluids.

Scent markers of Kieran's cum left her nose to twitch, while the saccharine smell of Omega slick left it running.

As if the wave of scent hit the Alpha just as hard, Kieran froze. Chest expanding on a deep breath, he brought her to slowly slide down his front, silently daring her to break eye contact once he'd caught her gaze.

Hard muscle, chest almost as broad as Caspian's. Male. He made certain her body felt the differences between them and didn't seem to care about the smears of dirt and fluids she'd left in her wake.

He might not have even noticed, glaring as he was.

So much anger lay naked in those green eyes, the threat of violence simmering on the surface. And what did he see in her gaze?

Wren could not even begin to imagine.

A brave Omega who had come to demand restitution for her boys? Probably not. Her body had yet to fully come down from Caspian's influence. Most likely her pupils were still partially blown. Open invitation as far as Alphas went.

But did he see how world-weary she was under the haze?

How thirsty? Starved? Lonely?

Did he see that she was frightened, but not of him?

Or did the Second Alpha only see a nameless Omega to expend his personal frustrations upon?

The silent back and forth between them ended

when her toes touched ground. Under her, was discarded laundry.

Something moist.

The distraction was all it took to snap her out of the foolishness of meeting, of challenging, an Alpha's gaze.

Lowering her eyes, she couldn't help the sound that escaped her lips when she saw what he had placed her upon.

Familiar fabric she had loved, rescued from rot, and sewn into her best dress. And it was covered in another woman's slick. Crusted, as if used repeatedly to wipe a spent cock upon.

Crumpled and discarded.

He'd had his new mate wear it. Wear *her* dress when Kieran had thought she was dead. A mate that had been made to look like her. Who had been ordered to be silent.

And though she should have shored herself up better, been stronger, her heart broke a little for Kieran in that moment.

These were not the actions of an ambivalent male. Her loss had caused him grief.

Grief expended foolishly, if the state of the room was any indication.

This male had no idea how to process emotion. None of the Alphas did. But Toby was correct; Kieran was the most broken.

And now he would break her in retribution.

While he did it, he'd crave empathy, he'd secretly scream for compassion. He wouldn't understand why he felt the things he did, and he would blame her for the discomfort of wretchedness.

This man, the one who had spent a week fucking a stranger who looked like her, was beyond saving.

And that—that one horrible notion—was what made her eyes sting.

Before he might see and misunderstand, Wren stepped back.

Her foot never landed. Wrist caught in a flash of male grip, Kieran held her still, pinned her with the anger in his tone. "Where do you think you're going?"

Each gaze a little more naked, more exposed, their eyes met again.

She let herself really see him, not just his position as Second Alpha. Deeper than his physical perfection, under the chiseled lines of his face and the cocky arrogance he used as a shield, he was bare.

No longer brilliant, the male's green eyes had dulled since last she'd seen him. Bloodshot and sunken, he looked even more tired than she felt. Sallow, unsmiling. Miserable.

A creature—if the astringent smoke and the

lingering scent of rotting food in the air were any indication—determined to self-destruct.

What haunted his gaze was a look she'd seen enough times to know. That look he thought he hid behind disdain and narrowed eyes.

Heartbreak.

It was the look all children abandoned to the Warrens had etched into their features before it sunk in that they would never get out. Most died still wearing it.

Alec had been unable to smile for years.

Mikael still harbored a ghost of early pain.

Those they trusted most abandoned them—whether through death, through deceit, or through neglect.

A fraction of Kieran's past was known to Wren, and that small sip had been more than enough for this man to be intimately acquainted with those sticky, unrelenting feelings. But for an Alpha of his stature to indulge them...

He was in agony.

For the rest of her days, Wren would hate the woman who had birthed and abused this male. The female who had essentially created the monster unleashed on the city.

Hate was infectious, yet there was nothing to do for it. She'd already spent years hating those responsible for throwing her kids into the mud.

And though she was not a violent woman, she'd slaughter every last one of them if they tried to harm her kids again.

Including this man who had slipped her boy a healing boost. She'd kill Kieran with her bare hands if he set so much as a violent finger on Alec… who was so much like him it turned her stomach.

There was nothing to do for it.

Not while both of them were trapped and haunted by what they were, how they had failed, mistakes they had made, and what life had fashioned them to be.

She was a mother, and he was an abandoned child who'd grown up loveless.

She was Omega. Kieran was Alpha.

It could be that plain and simple.

Tall as he was, staring down his nose at her in an obvious stance of superiority, Wren chose not to reach upward and stroke his hair the way that quieted his thoughts.

She might have squeezed his shoulder, touched over his heart.

Instead, her fingers brushed the buttons of his shirt, fumbling to undo them while still holding a burning gaze. An intake of air, held, was the male's only response before her hands slunk between fabric and flesh. Skimming fingertips over the rippling muscle of his flank, she hooked her arm around his torso, and pulled herself closer.

The hug was selfish on her part.

Wren needed his support, his superior strength, and a moment to prepare herself.

She was so filthy next to his freshly scrubbed skin, and though she knew it was no fault of her own, she felt ashamed.

He should have been the one ashamed, bringing her here to use her in the ruined nest of another woman. He should have been ashamed for dressing up his doll in her handmade frock.

He should have been on his knees begging her to forgive him.

But they both knew it would be her on her knees. Sucking him off. Being mounted from behind. Forced to kneel.

She held him tighter.

Kieran didn't purr, not while he exuded the acrid stink of impending violence, so she did. And the light rumble offered her some small measure of comfort.

Like his warmth.

His presence.

The fact he had yet to tear her away.

Had she the ability to speak, she would have whispered secrets to him—shared those little private moments that made this hellish life bearable. She would have comforted the broken child who worked the limbs of a man's body. She would have rebuked this recent behavior, and broken the fogged pipe stinking of spent drugs she could clearly see lying on the bed.

Having made the Warrens her home, Wren didn't miss the black dust he'd packed it with, the burn marks on furniture and blankets where he'd set it down after sucking poisoned air deep into his body.

The worst kind of drug to dull the greatest type of pain.

And high, he'd bitten that girl.

A thing she knew the male regretted, and that the doll would most likely suffer for.

Cheek to his chest, Wren held him all the harder and took in the chaos of the room.

If a space might reflect the owner's mental state, the big room was Kieran from head to foot.

Filthy.

Used.

Scattered with leavings.

Her shoulders shook and the male shoved her away, barking, as if the tone might hide the tremor in his voice. "Drink water first. There's food over there."

Stacked trays, old plates, half-eaten things the

population of the Warrens would be desperate to eat, moldered atop the room's desk.

She stared at it but made no move to walk through the mess.

"What? Do you want me to hand feed you, or something?" Anger brought the wrong kind of light to his eyes. "Move!"

It wasn't just that she didn't trust her legs, she didn't trust herself at all. Wren stood her ground.

Or she would have had a wet cough not stolen her forced bravado.

Before she might compose herself, he had her by the elbow. Rushing her through the carnage, he dragged her into an equally messy bathroom, and bent her over the sink.

Without being told, she angled her head under the spout, sucking down cold, trickling water between rattling pants of breath. Somewhere between the fifth swallow, the clump working its way from her lungs broke free.

Spitting it against the basin, she saw the same thing Kieran did.

Blood.

That's what broke him.

"You'd rather die in the Warrens, choking on shit, than be here?" His question, though spoken softly, was so very angry.

And instantly, so was she.

Pushing off from the sink, letting bloody phlegm swirl down the drain in a parade of clean water, Wren wiped the back of her mouth on her arm.

Yes, his life had been hard.

But she'd lost her family.

She'd lost her innocence.

She'd lost her home.

And she was going to slowly lose her life to mud and fetid air.

No one—NO ONE—*wanted* to exist in the Warrens

Chest heaving, Wren turned her back on him and went back to swallowing water.

Gathering her ratted hair in his fist as if to hold it for her to drink, Kiran held her skull under his power.

He could have flung her across the room for her insolence. He could have stoppered the sink and drowned her in the basin. But he just held tight, watching while she sucked down water like an animal.

And then his fingertips traced over the healing scratches on her back.

Scratches he had put there fucking her against the wall of her home, knotting her atop a pile of refuse, and pinning her down in the night to keep her warm.

20

———

Skin pricking, stomach near bursting from the amount of water hastily guzzled down, a shiver passed over Wren.

It was *his* touch. The way the edge of blunt nails dragged down her spine. How he released a possessive low hum under his breath.

Kieran intensified the awkward moment, his words distant, as if he spoke to himself. "Is what Toby claimed true? Even though they cast you off, you came back for your mates?"

Both Toby and Caspian might have marked her, both might have possessed some sort of intention toward her, but neither was a mate. *A bite mark didn't make a mate.*

Love, trust, and mutual respect did.

Toby may have wanted her forever, but Wren

suspected that any Omega female might have served his need to bond. Yes, he'd taken the time to learn her language. But he had also used what she'd taught him to manipulate all those around him. He'd beaten her boy, and he'd lied.

It had been his hand that had flung her into the mud before his guards. Where was his kindness then? Where was his mercy? How about his love? Wren almost snorted at the thought.

Delusional male; one she was so angry with, she had no idea how she'd stomach his body rutting into her.

And Caspian? The First Alpha had already told her he'd set her free upon estrous. This half-formed *bond* was just some experiment—an oddity for the First Alpha to experience between knotting the myriad of women in his pen. More importantly, unlike Toby, Caspian would not have bitten her had she not excited him in the frenzy of her violence. He truly didn't want her, not when it tarnished his infamy.

Caspian merely made the best of a bad situation and his slip in judgment—he used her for his personal indulgence, fully prepared to sever ties.

No, she had not returned here for her *mates*.

Sighing, trying her damnedest to dismiss the shudders Kieran's fingertips still drew from her flesh, Wren shook her head.

Still bent over the sink, resting her weight against the basin, she glanced through the mess of her hair. No longer did Kieran cut the image of anger. In fact, he seemed abnormally settled when he met her eyes, smeared in her dirt, as he was.

There was a clarity to his next question that was very unlike the frivolous and cruel Second Alpha. "You could have run away… avoided us, but you came back here. Why?"

It seemed he was expecting a grand statement, but Wren hardly knew where to begin.

Ran to where? The Warrens was vast, but not endless. She didn't have access to the upper levels or any way out of the city without a great deal of money to bribe the guards at the gate.

Pushing up, Wren straightened and let the man get a good long look at her—bare, dirty, dripping fluids, and clearly unhealthy. It was pointless to sign to him, he wouldn't understand. So, squeezing filth from her hair, she muddied her fingers, and smeared them over the cracked white subway tiles that coated the wall at her back, writing:

My boys.

A hint of evil in his smirk, a flare of light in green eyes. "You think we'd give them back to you?"

Throat bobbing, Wren swallowed, incapable of answering.

"Did Toby lie? You didn't know Caspian was searching for you?"

A single, subtle shake of her head.

"Because he threw you out. You thought he was done."

A nod.

"And you came anyway..." Crossing his arms over his chest, Kieran cocked his head. "You must have suspected he'd most likely kill you."

A debt was a debt, yet she'd come expecting it to be her last day. She'd swam through filth anticipating her body would be tossed right back into the sewage to rot. Not once did she figure Caspian would want her back. Turning to the wall, she pressed one hand to her heart, and pointed again at the two words that summed up her entire motivation.

My boys.

"You wasted your chance to be free." Kieran's next words fell with an odd ring. They fell unsure, as if what he shared he didn't wish to. "Before you get your hopes up, know that you won't find your kid here. Alec is gone."

That couldn't be right...

Eye twitched, her breath stopped mid exhale. Alec couldn't be gone! Caspian assured her he'd live, and that was even before Kieran had slipped the boy a healing boost.

Had they disposed of him when she was no longer here to entertain them? Had they hurt him?

"I didn't say he was dead, Omega. I said he was *gone*." The Second reached out to stop her wobbly forward assault, giving her a rough shake when her stray hand landed a pathetic slap to his chest. "Toby took your boy to the upper levels to serve as a runner for his offices in Council. The psychopath wanted to honor your memory."

Eyes wide and spilling fresh tears, Wren tried to find the world under her feet.

Toby got her boy out of the Pipeworks? Even though he thought she was dead?

He did that *for her*.

Upper levels? Clean air. No mud. Food on every street corner…

Head falling against Kieran's chest, Wren began to sob. And immediately the male misunderstood.

"I bet you wish you'd hidden now." Dropping his hold, he let her sink to the floor and stepped back as if she disgusted him.

The fraying threads that held her mentally together snapped. Just like that.

One moment she had a purpose, the next her purpose was served.

Alec was in the upper levels, safe, where he could take care of himself better than anyone might imagine. Even without her, he'd thrive. Now that he was no longer blind to what Caspian could and would do to the both of them, he'd sharpen up. He'd know when to run, and Wren was sure, if that kid put his mind to it, not even the Syndicate would find him.

Her child was rebellious, unruly, and completely underestimated by these bad men.

And Toby had unleashed him upon the upper levels.

Cracking, as if her body was stone and she was about to shed that craggy old skin, the weight just fell off of her.

And she cried all the harder for it. Right there, on the floor. Emotional vomit purged until she began to laugh.

Mikael was going to heal. Alec was safe.

And where did that leave her?

Shouldering a terrible new feeling—gratitude toward Toby.

She *appreciated* Toby for doing something self-less, felt in that moment a flicker of fondness the insane Third Alpha didn't deserve. Unsure if she'd be able to reconcile how much she loathed him for whipping her boy with how much she adored him for taking Alec from this horrible place, she put her forehead to the floor.

After an embarrassing length of time, her mind ceased reeling, and she was able to push back to her haunches. Twisting so her legs splayed before her, Wren leaned against the coolness of the wall, breathless and… smiling.

This must be what it felt like to die.

A lightness that fooled her body into believing it drifted, not slumped on dirty tiles. She couldn't even smell the mud and shit that she'd crawled through.

Not when out of nowhere Kieran leaned over her, so close that if she turned her head just a touch, she could lay her cheek to his.

Before she might lean into his heat and draw in his scent, the male shoved to his feet. Bracing his legs on either side of her hips, he tore down his zipper, and shoved a fully hard cock past her teeth. Unprepared, Wren instinctively swallowed against the rising water that was moments from escaping her belly, and found his pelvis met her lips.

In all the times this demon had worked his evil down her throat, he'd never shoved his meat so deep.

Not that she particularly noticed.

She couldn't even comprehend the words he was shouting as he held himself there beyond her ability to hold her breath.

Kieran keened, jaw clenched and teeth exposed in the following hiss.

What shot into her belly warmed soul-deep,

shooting zings of feeling from tummy to fingertips. *Filled her*.

Becoming an active participant to the mauling, Wren swallowed again, and set her teeth to the root of his cock. Should he pull away what fed her, she'd bite down. Hold him until she'd had her fill.

More and more flowed thick and creamy from him to her, bloated her belly, yet still she refused to let go.

Rough fingers pinched her jaw, forcing it apart. "You have to breathe!"

The entire length of him was drawn from her esophagus, slimed with her mucus, and pulsating as it continued to spurt on her parted lips and waiting tongue.

But it wasn't cum.

Thick, viscus, and white as snow. Stringy like taffy.

Addictive.

A nutrient substance rutting Alphas fed their Omegas in estrous when females were unable to eat.

When they could hardly drink.

A substance that would tax the Alpha's strength as he gave his vigor to his female.

Something Kieran could have only been able to produce if he'd been with an estrous high Omega.

He'd force-fed Wren another woman's due. And

she, the slut that she was, lapped it down like ambrosia.

Immediately buoyed, feeling reason and strength return, the panting Omega met burning green eyes and knew.

Kieran had lied.

21

Lightly laughing at a mildly funny quip, Rosie kept her face bright, her smile winning, and let the Alpha who'd pulled her to his lap think he was the only man in the world. Twirling his hair around her finger, easing close enough the sweetness of Omega scent might charm him, she drew in a decent option for nightly protector.

Someone who would keep her out of the orgy in his greed to have Omega cunt to himself.

This game, she'd played it a million times. Same smile, same giggle, different cock.

Play the part, and food and water were available in abundance—as was a sort of safety. The protection of strong males, the comradery of other females who lived and breathed the same sorry life. Everything in the pen was organized and in its box.

But it was a job. Unpaid even.

Generally, Caspian gave his whores everything they needed beyond the standard food, shelter, water. Spoiled them as far as pimps went with clothing, luxury items, even the occasional excursion into the city. He didn't beat them, not unless they had it coming.

But he sure as fuck didn't care about them either.

The male liked holes. Preferred those holes to be of the female variety and trained in how to make his dick cough up cum like a geyser.

And that male was going to hand her off to whichever asshole brought his missing mouse in. Which, considering the Warrens, could be fucking anyone.

And when she was handed off, the future she had tried so hard to build would crumble. Aside from the upscale bride markets, the pen was the nicest place an Omega might whore. Here there was an actual chance she could be sold to some powerful old fart who lived above the smog.

Where she would get to have babies and be safe. Even if the Alpha was weak and wanted nothing more than a sexy nursemaid, he'd be able to afford guards. Life would be comfortable.

But all these years she hadn't been offered in trade. Not while she was one of Caspian's top girls.

She hadn't been offered anything but more work on her back.

And time was running out.

The mouse was alive; Rosie's days were numbered.

A sense of sadness she had refused to allow herself to feel in all the years she'd been in the pen was knocking on her heart for entry.

So she smiled all the harder, moaned all the louder, and faked orgasms like a fucking pro.

At this point, she could slick her thighs on demand—do the ol' in-out-in-out, and feel nothing. Because she'd had a plan and a future.

Now she had an ax over her head and a replacement who hadn't even had to brave the pen, the males, or the females.

No. Jax only had to contend with three.

Well, Toby was a freak on a whole other level, but still. Three only. Rosie had fucked three guys before breakfast.

After all, those who didn't fuck didn't thrive.

Turn the men down, refuse to participate, and starve.

And it was so much more than the lack of food. The girls would turn on those who took but didn't give. Share the burden of pleasing the males, share the disappointment and the shame, or get your throat cut while you slept. Ladies didn't get to languish in the pen. Period.

Those who tried to hide away, the men forgot. Once the men forgot, no one would notice a corpse. In all this water they just… floated away.

And new pussy came.

A gruff, unpracticed purr seasoned the words, "What do you think about that, beautiful?"

Rosie had no fucking clue what the man had said. Not that it mattered, she knew the perfect coy look, the tease of expectant smile he'd want to see at the corner of her lips. She didn't need to speak at all.

Even Caspian fell for that one time and again.

But before she might make her play, might cuddle closer and put all she was on offer, high pitched, unintelligible shrieking cut through the room's many conversations.

A spitting, clawing, pale-haired mess of an Omega was dumped on the floor by Caspian's personal guard.

Rosie's heart stopped. This was it; this was her end.

The mouse had been found.

And a tear fell, unbidden and strange over a painted cheek before someone as hard-hearted as her might will it away.

What had been loud grew silent, couples in the

midst of flirtation, conversation, fucking, stopped long enough to see the white-haired female gain her footing.

Thrusting a tangle of hair away from her face, the girl wobbled forward as if she thought to pursue the very Alphas who'd caged her in. "She can't have him! Kieran is MY MATE!"

The lurch and first beat of a heart kicking back in jolted Rosie forward. Wiping the back of her hand over her cheek before that sorry droplet might betray her to anyone, she gawped—just like everyone else—at the wild thing daring to threaten Alphas.

"My mate will have you killed! Do you hear me? Kieran will murder you for treating me this way!" As if to punctuate her threat, the doll, the very doll whom Rosie had taken such exception to last week, set her marked shoulder on display.

This wasn't a mouse.

The *not mouse* turned to the room, to the spectators who'd broken character. "She harassed me! Told them I was ugly, that they didn't want me. Claimed I copied her… as if she invented Omegas!"

Oh, and now it was getting good. Rosie might be at her end—she wasn't stupid, she knew exactly what this cunt was blathering about. After all, she'd been recently replaced herself. But there could be something here to work with.

Slipping off the Alpha's lap, Rosie approached, all class. "Who called you that, sugar?"

A breakdown of epic proportions began before Rosie's blue eyes.

"I did everything he wanted." The doll, the fresh meat, fell to her knees and sobbed. "Nothing she said was true. She slandered me, right in front of him. She told lies!"

The show was glorious, so believable that only a few of the whores laughed under their breath.

But a few was all it took to set the broken doll into another rage.

Again, the new Omega pulled her hair aside to show the mark on her shoulder. And it was true, she stank of Kieran's spend, her slick, and god only knows what else. "He's my mate. MINE! She can't have him."

"Honey." And that endearment came like honey, thick and sweet. "No male here is faithful. It's no fault of yours. I mean, look at you. Pretty as a sunset from the top tier."

"She harassed me! In front of my mate." More tears, real ones which said so much more about this female than any of the crazy things she'd screamed.

"Who? I'll talk to her."

Wiping her runny nose, the Omega looked up. Those helpless wide eyes had probably got her far in life. "He called me his doll."

For fuck's sake. Rosie swallowed, about ready to reach forward and shake the story from this woman. "Did she have white hair?"

"Yeah."

"And she *said* things about you to your male?"

Defensive, all claws, the doll hissed. "That's what I said, isn't it?"

The laughter in the room grew.

"Cupcake, I hate to be the bearer of bad news."

"Yeah?"

"If you want to be angry, be angry with Kieran. Hell, we all have been one time or another. He promised me children and a way out of this hellhole." Rosie pointed to an exotic Beta who'd been here even longer than she had. "He promised to clear Janice's debts and a job up top somewhere respectful. All of us have been let down by Kieran. Life is disappointment, especially around here." Not an appropriate thing to announce in front of the clients, but at this point, who cared? Rosie was toast, burnt toast covered in cum jelly with zero fucks left to give. "You're in the pen now, just like the rest of us. Pick a John and get to work. Cock ain't gonna suck itself."

The slight thing straightened her shoulders and squared off against the queen of the whores. "I'm mated. I don't have to fuck anyone anymore."

Boy, was this new girl in for a rough go of it.

"Suit yourself, doll. But just so you know? The Omega you saw, the one Caspian marked? She's Toby's mate. And, sugar... she can't talk."

Tossing her bleached hair, the Omega turned to walk out, screeching again when the guard at the door shoved her right back in. Landing on her ass, humiliated when the Alpha guard barked, "Stay in the pen!" she went wild.

Forearm clawed, a few beads of blood matting the dark hair, said Alpha gave her the only warning that might shut up the whimpers and whines. "And if I hear you sass Rosie again, I'll throw you to the slaves for the night's entertainment."

22

Under the warm cascade of clean water, Kieran scrubbed her skin as if he were on a mission to scour off any trace of what had happened in the big room. Every inch of her was washed, rinsed, washed again, until Wren's flesh was pink from too much friction.

He cleaned her ears as if she were a child, wiped her nostrils free of mud despite her attempts to bat his hand away.

Perfectly capable of cleaning her own body, she tolerated only so much.

But her complaints were weak, unspoken, and considering she could hardly stay standing without his support, pointless.

Soap, shampoo, special cleansers designed specifically for an Omega—every bit of foamy lathering chemicals was used up, even after the water no longer ran brown with dirt.

Yet it would seem that whatever he was determined to get off of her, was more than skin deep.

And Wren, she couldn't meet the male's eyes after what he'd done, how she'd swallowed, and still craved more. Had even dared to fight him under that spray when the urge took him again— when he'd pushed her to her knees and thrust his cock between her lips until she swallowed his full length. Then he filled her belly with sustenance.

Three times so far, he'd invaded her throat.

Three times he'd given her his Alpha nutrient substance.

At each of the interludes, it seemed something had completely come over the male. He practically shook with the need to force his ejaculate down her gullet.

And she was no better, once fed something akin to a drug. A single taste, and Wren went from fighting the Alpha to keep his erection from her lips, to fighting him to keep his cock buried so far down her throat she couldn't breathe.

When he'd filled her, when her face was turning purple, he'd pinch her jaw and pull out, leaving her bent and sputtering, and too weak to drag him back for more.

And then the manic scrubbing began all over again.

Between her toes. Behind her ears. Eyelids. Navel. Labia.

Every trace of Caspian's scent was rinsed from inside her.

Wren had never seen Kieran in such a manic state—utterly focused, grim, determined. Where was the flippant snark, the disapproving looks, the teasing?

This male was someone utterly different.

And to be perfectly honest, he frightened her.

The silence, the roughness of his handling when she failed to turn *just so*. He moved her as if she were a thing, an item. He ignored how her knees knocked and made her lean into him each time she slipped.

It wasn't until exhaustion won out and she slumped to the floor, refusing to stand no matter how he snarled at her and tried to drag her upward, that he finally stopped.

Whatever he was planning to do, whatever the purpose for the insane washing, she just wanted him to do it and have it over.

The water cut off.

Arms scooped her off the slippery tile, and while she hung like a limp noodle, Kieran took her from the bathroom.

Leaving a trail of water droplets where they passed, the male surveyed the room, and let out a lengthy, irritated snarl. He kicked a nearby pile of old dishes, sending ceramic to smash into the wall, rotting food scattering for the rats no doubt hidden in the piles of garbage scattered/ heaped in the room.

Skin tight from too much scrubbing, Wren ignored most of his grumbled complaints, her attention instead on the soiled nest waiting on the bed. One brush of that soggy fabric would make her feel far filthier than the mud she'd sported over every inch upon her arrival.

Cringing, knowing it was inevitable, she let out a loud breath.

Kieran hiked her up higher in his arms, the swing of his head when he stopped surveying his disaster so abrupt her eyes went wide when they met his.

How he glared.

The man was fucking pissed. Snorting bull, steam rising from his ears, incensed.

Again, this was not Kieran. Not the man who secretly desired to be purred to and have his hair stroked. Not the walking open wound his mother left on his soul. This glaring male was Alpha only.

Lacked personality.

It had to be the aftereffects of whatever drugs he'd inundated himself with over the last few days.

Even with the shower, he looked more animal than man.

Wren signed best as she could one handed. *"You need to sleep it off."*

"That first day, you made your nest on the floor. Over there." Not breaking eye contact, he jerked his chin toward the window. "You'll make one there now."

With what? Every item in this room was disgusting.

Stomping over the refuse, he carried her to the least cluttered corner of the room. Before he set her bare feet to the floor, he kicked aside odds and ends, clearing a circle.

Still sopping wet, hair tangled and in need of a comb, Wren shivered once the male stepped back.

"If you move from that spot before I return, I will punish you."

Nodding, wary, arms around her middle, Wren complied.

And just like that, a fully naked and very wet Kieran charged from the room.

The door slammed, perhaps even more forcefully than upon their arrival, and Wren let out the breath she'd been holding.

Three beats of her heart passed before she

disobeyed his order. Rushing from the cleared circle, Wren dashed toward the food trays that seemed the most fresh, grabbing up random bits of abandoned food and shoving them into her mouth.

Taste didn't matter, texture, or smell. All that mattered was getting something into a body that was running on nothing.

Nothing but Kieran's nutrient ejaculate.

God help her, she didn't want to ever be sucked into the enrapturing high that thick fluid inspired again. It was wrong, so wrong, and if she could get her stomach to stop rumbling, perhaps the male would cease this craziness.

And that's how he found her upon his speedy return, picking through scraps like the Warrens rat she was.

She thought he'd been angry before…

That was nothing to the roaring male running full steam across the room.

FIST IN HER HAIR, long fingers down her throat, Kieran forced every bit of food she'd swallowed to come back up. Roughly gagging her despite tears and pleading moans to vomit up every bite.

The already dirty rug was ruined.

Putrid.

A string of mucus tying her fingers-stuffed-mouth to the mess, Wren heaved again. Over and over until there was nothing left to lose.

Slimy digits left her aching throat one second, and a resounding slap hit her rump the next. It was more startling than painful, at least at first. As the male continued to rail open-palmed punishment on her ass, discomfort burned into outright throbbing.

"What the hell is going on in here?"

She hadn't even registered the sound of the door being thrown open, not between her own noisy struggles to escape the fire Kieran affected upon her skin.

The Third's shouted fury changed nothing. More slaps fell on her rear.

Roaring with the same strength he used to chasten her flesh, Kieran bellowed, "When I left the room, the Omega disobeyed me and ate old food!"

Boots stomped over the debris, the Third approaching in full temper. "She's starving, Kieran!"

"Which is why I went to the kitchens to grab her something fresh. I brought her clean bedding and clothes." Not sure how he managed to do it, the Second's strikes fell even harder. "And I came back to find her swallowing drug-laced garbage!"

Wren couldn't see it, but she felt it in the jerk of

the man who'd somehow pinned her over his lap. Toby had caught Kieran's wrist.

No more slaps fell, still her backside burned as if set aflame.

"She can't take anymore, Kieran." Toby's soft spoken statement wasn't said with anger, which implied something Wren didn't want to consider. "Punish her, but not until she's had food, water, and rest. Hell, let Caspian be the one to do it if you really want to make a lasting impression. But right now, our little Omega is not well."

"The amount of Bliss Dust in that food would have killed even Caspian. It wasn't meant to be eaten all at once."

"Bliss Dust? Shit." With Kieran's fist still tangled in her wet hair, Wren couldn't raise her head, but she did watch Toby toe her pile of vomit. "You got it all out?"

"It couldn't have been in her longer than a minute." Kieran's arm must have been set free, for his hand palmed the stinging globe of her ass, the warmth of his palm increasing the pain.

"If Caspian finds out about this, he'll do far more than beat her ass red."

Drugged food? Kieran's words from earlier didn't make sense, not after what Wren had seen. Not after his cock had spilled that fluid down her throat.

She wasn't in estrous. Just high.

Before Wren could hold on to that shard of consciousness, a new sort of warmth sufficed her. The pain Kieran had brought upon her ebbed away, and listless, cloud-soft calm stole over.

Snot thickened snivels dried up. Her every muscle went limp.

When her lashes next parted, the blurred faces of Kieran and Toby hovered over her. She didn't even know when she'd been turned.

"Sunshine." The back of roughened male knuckles caressed her cheek, the man speaking as if disappointed in her. "Don't make us hurt you again."

How could anything in the world possibly hurt when everything felt so good? Just the feel of male skin on hers, the smell of potent Alphas, and Wren was in *bliss*.

"In a few hours you'll be fine." A devilish wink, and Toby smirked. "You sure are lovely when you smile, sweet girl."

The arms around her tightened, pulling her away from Toby's attention. "It's not your turn, Third. Piss off."

Though there was boiling irritation under the Third's grin, Toby backed off and raised his hands before him in capitulation. "By all means, Kieran. Just, clean her up before you fuck her silly."

The word *fuck* and Wren's insides clenched. The following rush of fluid that rushed from between her thighs obscene.

Toby's eyes dilated, the male visibly swallowing.

Kieran, still holding her in his arms, straightened to standing and challenged his pack mate. "I'm warning you, Third. I'm not in a sharing mood."

Grin growing, Toby took a few careful steps backward. "It seems that neither am I. So let's not scare her by ripping one another to shreds. I'll go, but only if you swear to me you'll feed her. We don't want our little Omega getting in any more trouble with all this garbage lying about."

Kieran's low, rusted growl moved through Wren's every cell. "Oh, I intend to feed her all right."

At the door, Toby seemed to be fighting himself to open the portal and leave. White-knuckled fist to the knob, he threw over his shoulder, "While you wash her off, I'll see that the room gets cleaned. We don't want another accident."

23

Blinking, the fuzzy glow inundating her line of sight began to slowly diminish. Belly to the warmth of another body, cradled in powerful limbs, Wren's world came into razor-sharp clarity.

Too sharp, the light streaming in through the room's windows glaring.

Under her, the musculature of an Alpha shifted —the male registering a change in the limp woman splayed and held over him.

He drew in a rib-expanding breath.

Wren, in tandem, exhaled, the pounding behind her eyes growing.

Her lashes swept down again, attention running over the muscled torso of her living pillow, past his naked hip to a hair-dusted thigh, to see that nothing was right beyond.

Nothing in that over-bright space looked familiar outside of a few sparse pieces of wooden furniture.

The big room.

It had been stripped down to the cement floors. The couches gone, the purple bunting and pillows gone, the garbage gone, the offensive smells… gone.

But one familiar scent did perfume the air, the Alpha markers that undoubtedly belonged to Kieran.

Far more viscid than the mud she'd waded through to enter the waterworks, her mental fog swirled murky, thick, and cloying.

The last thing she recalled was warm water, too much soap, and persistent hands scrubbing overly sensitized flesh. Then this, this stripped room, this extended contact with Kieran who only invited attention if he were the one being cradled. He never cradled, just like he never kissed.

Male lips pressed to her crown, reminding Wren of another time the Second betrayed his character. Her house; how he fucked her in the graveyard and kept her warm against the night's chill.

How he'd covertly given her boy the healing boost and threatened to kill her if she ever told.

This male had threatened her life often, had purposefully given her pain, had degraded her. So what had happened; what had he done? How had she gone from shower to gap in memory? How had the room gone from chaos to vacant?

The beat of his heart under her ear, the constant, sleepy thrum of an Alpha purr untangled her growing rush of adrenaline. Lifting an arm that weighed about a thousand pounds, Wren found moving far harder than it should have been. In fact, the wobbly effort upset her balance and almost sent her slipping bodily off Kieran's chest

Increasing the pressure of his hold around her body, Kieran gave her a warning growl. One that went unheard once Wren realized how incredibly dry her mouth had become.

Sticky, with a metallic residue slightly under-lined by the taste of Kieran.

Lavender eyes flowed to the bedside table where a glass of crystal clear water collected enough condensation to drip down and mark the wood.

She wanted to reach for it with a fervor, but her body felt so heavy.

Even so, her arm extended, missed the mark, and almost knocked the whole glass of precious, clean water onto the floor.

Before she might try again, Kieran stroked a

hand down her back, traveling the length of her spine until a meaty grip palmed her ass.

Jerking, a raw yelp wheezing from a parched throat upon unexpected pain, Wren shot up. Palms to his chest, eyes wide, she looked down to see Kieran cock a brow.

Relaxed and languid, he wore an expression as naked as their touching flesh. "Didn't you learn your lesson not to eat or drink things you found lying around?"

What the hell was he talking about?

Another firm grip of male palm squeezed her cheek, and again, a pained noise escaped her lips. Instinct moved her to look back, to see just why his hands brought about such pain, and Wren gasped to see the bruising all over her butt.

"You look so innocent, so put upon, for someone so guilty. Are you going to pretend that you don't remember?" The male who'd asked the question sounded entirely reasonable in tone, even though he continued to manipulate the black and blue globes of her ass specifically to cause discomfort.

Vague flashes of his cock down her throat, that nectar she could swallow forever running like honey into an empty belly.

Memory of unexpectedly gagging, a wet cough following the sudden extraction of the throbbing flesh pulled from her throat. Wren would have chased after it, had she not been restrained by the very man who'd pushed his way into her mouth.

A mix of want and mortification, flushed her skin pink, and Wren *remembered* so much more.

Kieran was pair-bonded to the doll.

He had fed her his nectar, over and over, despite her protests, and she had eaten food left in the room in an attempt to protect herself from his urges to feed her more.

The food had been drugged, and he had saved her life by forcibly extracting it from her stomach… then spanked her like a child.

"I don't care if you don't want me." Abandoning her ass, a warm caress moved up her spine until Kieran had gathered the hair at her nape in his fist. Drawing her close, his point razor sharp, he growled, "Do you understand that? You can say no, and I will still make you lie here. I'll still knot you until you beg for more. I'll use tricks that will leave you panting and on the brink of madness only I can soothe. I'll put my children in your belly."

The man was deluding himself. He was bonded to another. A full bond. Going against his urges to nest with his mate would torment him with every thrust he put in her body.

And children… no. Wren would not raise babies in this hellhole.

So she shook her head to make her point clear. It did nothing but add to the fire in the Second's green-eyed gaze.

In fact, her negation seemed only to excite him, the cock pressed between their bodies kicking with that first rush of blood. "If you ever disobey me again, if you stupidly put yourself in danger, I'll give you so much more than a bruised ass to worry about."

As she was between his spread thighs, there was little leverage she could use to sit up without pulling away, and it would seem he was not in a charitable mood. When she pressed against his chest, Kieran showed his teeth, eyeing her neck as if tempted to rip right into it.

Caspian had already marred that spot. Much of her flesh would forever be decorated by the First's attention. Looking to it brought the First Alpha to Kieran's thoughts. "Caspian would have hurt one of your boys, badly, to make a point. Keep that in mind next time you're tempted to disobey. Be grateful that I am not going to tell him what took place here."

Her disobedience had not been intentional, Wren had just been so hungry, so frantic to stop falling into the spell of the fluid Kieran kept flooding into her belly. Not at all in her right mind.

"Had I not returned as quickly as I had, *you would have died.* Do you have any idea what an overdose on Bliss Powder looks like? Bloody foam spills out your mouth, bulging eyes, the skin turns a mildew shade of green in less than a few hours."

How could she have known all that food had been drugged? He'd pointed it out to her. And why the heck had he been feeding it to the *new little girl*? All the females here wanted Kieran. He didn't need to—

"I found dear ol' mom like that. Dress up around her waist, mouth gaping, and reeking of whatever pimp she'd got the drugs from. Man probably works for me now. I wouldn't have any way of knowing which one of my pushers was there with her when she took it too far."

Inner rant cutting short, Wren felt the real-world weight of those words. She felt them, imagining finding her own mother in such an awful state, knowing that the person partially responsible probably called him boss. That Kieran knowingly had his men concoct, push, and sell designer drugs despite his history.

The feelings that came with all of that were so ugly she didn't even know what to call them.

What if Alec had seen her that way? What if they had shown Mikael? What if either of them were ever tempted with this shit. Heck, Alec might be upstairs, but he was and always would be a member of The Syndicate. Part of his job would be to push their interests.

Sometimes it was easy to forget just what these males were really responsible for.

Trying to clear the sand from her throat, Wren found she couldn't meet Kieran's eyes. He'd see the judgment, the pity, all the things he hated most. So she rolled into him in the only movement he'd allow, the meat of her palm to her eye, and he settled her frame where he wished.

And she purred, as much to comfort herself as to appease him.

Gentle fingers combed through her clean, dry hair. "If you think purring over me is going to make this better, you're wrong."

The censure of her glare behind her hand, the silent *not-everything-is-about-you* look, she kept them to herself. Yet the way her purr magnified as if in defense of her feelings, didn't stop him from batting aside her hand and drawing her mouth up for a kiss.

Chaste, lingering. Soft and gentle.

A lover's kiss.

Fingertips burrowing against her scalp in a way that left her tingling, he pulled her small body ever nearer. Thighs parted, legs moved with ease, until he'd rolled her under his mass, all the while his mouth working magic, his purr infiltrating, and his cock growing ever harder.

Silken lips moved to her ear. "I could have fucked you the whole time you were high. You begged for it with those pleading eyes and parted lips. It was all I could do just to restrain you. Remember that. I could have fucked you raw, done anything. But I didn't."

On that score, he wasn't lying. Wren's memories of the past hours were nothing but flashes of slick and aching need. She'd been a bitch in heat, rubbing this man, squealing and whining in frustration as he denied her.

Is that what estrous would feel like?

A brainless need for physical release no matter who was near? An embarrassment of invitations and a drooling mouth?

That's what Alphas were eager to enjoy? It seemed so mechanical, passionless in every important way.

The tip of Kieran's tongue flicked between her lips, a small grunt coming from the male when his cock spilled on her belly in invitation.

When more fluid burst from him, more than was normal to entice a female, when it began to run down her sides and pool on the fresh sheets, Wren realized he'd cum fully. Just from a kiss.

He'd denied himself a knot, would be in aching

discomfort unless pressure was applied, but did not draw her hands down. He didn't make her do anything but continue to bear his mouth.

Breathless, a hair's breadth from her parted lips, Kieran caught her eyes before she might be wise enough to look away. What confused her most was reflected in those envy-green eyes. Affection.

"Drink the cup of water, it's safe. There is more in a pitcher under the table. We'll build a nest when you're finished. When it's done, you will invite me to share it."

He had not offered any threats. There had been no bet or temptations. These direct orders without caveats were so unlike him.

But welcome.

"Are you hungry?"

Always. The wry smirk that came with the thought was enough to explain. The rumble of her stomach sealed it.

Climbing over her body to straddle her face, Kieran slipped halfway into the creature he'd been in the shower. Cock already pumping nutrient substance so that it dangled like a thick dollop of cream, he smeared her lips before she could protest. "Then open up."

He was down her throat before Wren even registered the turn.

More than he had offered her yet drained from

him to nourish her, to cut off her air, to set her sex to dripping. As with every other time he'd forced himself on her this way, he had to fight her off to retrieve his member, and left her panting, red-faced, and confused.

When she scooched back, fighting her breath and her body's reaction, her feet slipped on the copious slick unintentionally spilled.

Easing back, Kieran took her chin and looked over her blush. "Did you think I offered you food?"

Of course that's what she thought!

He lifted the cup, holding it out to her and helping her keep it steady so she might gulp it down. Clean water rinsed the addictive taste of him from her mouth, but it did not wash away her desire to lean forward and lick his oozing cockhead for another taste.

Palming his erection, expression blank, Kieran subtly waved his cock at her. "Do you want more?"

Yes! But she sure as hell was not going to latch on.

A shaking hand set the cup on the table, an extended troubled breath falling from her lips as she slipped from the bed as if to reach for the pitcher. The inelegant retreat was allowed. Glass refiled, drained, and filled again, she took all the water she could bear.

Next came the building of a nest. One built around the male already occupying it.

After an inordinate amount of time, long after the nest was truly finished and she was just fiddling to stall, Kieran took her hand, and shook his head as if to say *no more*.

Pulling her in, he arranged her comfortably on her back, her legs cradling his hips. And then, like a total stranger, he spent hours making careful love to her.

All of it was about her pleasure, every touch seeking out the places on her body that made the Omega sing.

Not an ounce of pain came even in the moments his long thrusts became more passionate. He didn't twist her into a pretzel or mock her lack of skill. Instead he praised her with soft compliments and gratuitous attention.

Wound up beyond the euphoria of a mating high, Wren lost all sense of time. Waves of pleasure washed away regret, purified fear, and purged anger. When at long last he knotted her, she was an active participant, kissing her lover, pulling him nearer, enraptured and enwrapped in the form of a doting Alpha.

She didn't even notice when he set his teeth to the other side of her neck, floating far away and lost in a sense of joy. The pain didn't even register when Kieran punched his teeth deep.

It wasn't until she woke later, still in their nest, still in his arms, to the sounds of a holo projected before them that she even smelled the blood.

Kieran, watching a comedy, had one arm thrown behind his head, laughing as if all was right and normal.

24

Fingering the tight collar of her dress, hooking fabric away from her throat as if that might make it easier to breathe, Wren plodded after the fast-moving Alpha dragging her through the halls. Kieran had her by the wrist, walking with an air of menace so unlike him, snarling at any who passed, that she could hardly keep up.

Twice she had tripped over her feet and the long skirt tangling about her ankles. Twice she had barely managed not to face-plant into the concrete.

Both times Kieran righted her, cast a glare about, and immediately continued the relentless pace.

The journey from the big room to Caspian's den was not so far, but by the time they reached the catwalk soaring over churning waters below, Wren was winded.

Before them waited the crossing.

She hated this part, walking over the rusted metal bridge, the drop down visible and stomach-churning.

But before she could steel herself to brave the crossing, an arm swept under her. Snagged to the Alpha's chest, breath knocked from her body, three large, male strides later and they were before the guarded portal.

And then she was back on her feet, her constrictive dress straightened by the same male who'd chosen it.

He'd spent at least ten minutes buttoning up the tiny row of seed pearls that held it closed from her navel to her throat. This was after the ridiculous amount of time he'd taken cleaning and treating the pointless bite mark on her throat.

Pointless since *there was no bond between them.* There couldn't be. Kieran was bonded to another.

Yet, utterly self-indulgent, he purred grandly as he brushed back her hair to admire it. He licked at the scabbed wounds, smiled, and in the privacy of the big room, was wholly playful when he nipped.

Wren, already covered in claiming marks from Caspian and Toby, tried to consider it just another scar, but *this* mark out of all of them disturbed her.

Because it had meaning beyond its pointlessness.

And that meaning was wrong.

Imagining other females seeing it and laughing, knowing that no bond of any sort might give it credibility, she felt like a fraud.

Yet she still came on Kieran's cock when he took her… again.

She still returned his passion and his caress.

And his kiss.

Culpable for her part in the charade, she'd counted down the minutes until Toby might come and take his turn. For once, she craved the Third's presence, as if he might fix all of this, crack one of his rude jokes, and set her at ease despite his unhinged mental state.

But Toby never came.

She did. She came over and over between long naps and meals of Alpha nutrient cum.

There had been no real food, only Kieran to sustain her—the Alpha draining his own vigor to bolster hers.

Then… Caspian commanded her presence. She'd heard the summons, taken aback by the irritation snarled from Kieran's wrist communicator.

"Deliver her, Kieran. NOW!"

That was it. Four words followed by the Second

throwing an empty water glass across the room to shatter.

To say Wren was startled was an understatement.

In that moment, gone was any ease between them. In that moment, gone was the Kieran he had pretended to be.

As if he finally realized the sham. As if he felt the lack of connection register, and instead of regret, it was anger clouding green eyes.

"You shouldn't have hid in the mud. Why didn't you come back to me?" Sweeping tangled tawny hair from his forehead, he snarled. "I helped your boy!"

Guilt did not belong in her heart, but it snapped at her all the same. Much stronger than the guilt was her own deeply planted resentment. *I want my children back. I want a place where they can grow up and not die. They are the only reason I would come to this place.*

"I can't understand you."

That makes two of us.

"What do you want from me?"

Why did he have to look so wounded, as if she had done something to earn such a sorry expression?

There was no answer she could give, lavender eyes falling to the wayside as her fingertip knocked against her breastbone. It made a hollow sound.

Which was fitting.

Still, she offered a shake of her head, softening it with a hint of tired smile before looking back at the looming male. *Caspian is waiting.*

And Caspian waited for no man. Not even for his Second.

Nor did he take other male's leavings. She was to be clean of other scents before he used her. Yet when she entered the bathroom, Kieran refused to allow her access to the shower.

The First, who already sounded angry, would not approve.

Wren signed, knowing Kieran didn't understand, but hoping the sentiment translated. She told him that she needed to wash.

"No." Indulgent, sweet, Kieran had been replaced with a snappish Alpha who wore a thickly disapproving glare.

Anticipating the mountain of insults that always partnered that look, Wren sucked in a breath.

But he said nothing.

Nothing at all while he drew her back to the bedroom and dressed her in tense silence—in new clothing that still smelled of the factory it was made in. It was a fragrance Wren had forgotten existed, and one sniff brought childhood memories rushing back. Once upon a time, she'd had a full belly, clean clothing, water, even a place to hide from her father most days.

She'd had a mom who did her best.

A mom Wren had missed in all the years she'd been slowly sinking into the mud.

Who could imagine that something so simple as the smell of new clothes would be so powerful?

In the armoire before her, everything was new, the old dresses shared by the women of the pen gone.

And this new dress… was modest.

It covered her from wrist to chin. It covered the same wound on her throat that it chafed.

A comforting change from endless nudity and the sort of costumes the males had hung from her shoulders before. Yet again, something Caspian would take exception to. His bite marks were covered. His claiming mark on her throat encased in the same fabric that hid Kieran's mistake.

Kieran led Wren from the room, and almost immediately, they happened upon Rosie in the halls.

The blue-eyed beauty took one look at the garment and her composure slipped. "Kieran, I need—"

The Second brushed her aside, never breaking step. "Not now, Rosie."

Following, the blonde Omega tried to grab at his arm. "Please, Kieran. I'm begging you. If I was ever anything to you, speak for me. Don't let him give me to whoever brought her back."

Snarling, an animal bark forcing the woman off, Kieran didn't break pace.

Wren did, that was the first time she tripped, looking back at a crushed woman who stank of real distress.

When their eyes met, it shook her.

The whole last hour shook her.

And now the door to Caspian's den was swinging open.

25

———

Seated in the chair Wren had come to recognize as Caspian's favorite, the First Alpha slowly turned his head their direction. Kieran was not spared so much as a glance—not when all of Caspian's attention was devouring her alive.

The dress…

Without so much as a hint of alteration to his expression, she could tell he *hated* it. But it also intrigued him for what it might stand for.

Of the three of them, this male most preferred to see his marks upon her pale skin, so he might touch, remember, and enjoy. Dressed as she was, it would require effort for him to reach what he believed he owned.

Though he most likely would rip the garment

off, that in itself might amuse him. From the glow in his eyes, Wren was certain that very thought crossed his mind.

He would enjoy it.

Until he saw what was hidden underneath. And Caspian would see them, both the bite mark and the bruising on her rear.

"There is food for you on the table, pretty mouse."

Food that smelled of heaven.

Wren would have fallen upon the offerings, eaten with abandon, but Kieran still had a hold of her wrist, stopping her excited momentum forward with grip of iron. Stiff, the Second growled lowly, and seemed to fight his impulse to yank her back to his side.

Caspian saw it all, yet still his face remained impassive. Still he kept to his great chair.

Eyeing the abundant spread, enough mouthwatering dishes waiting to feed an army, Wren yanked lightly on her arm.

Muscle in his jaw ticking, it clearly took Kieran a great deal of effort to lift his fingers one at a time from her wrist. And off she went to the table, impatient to be free of the Second, eager to have an excuse not to look upon the First, but mostly famished.

Pastries and meat—*steaming meat* seasoned

with herbs. Root vegetables, salads, sauces, all the decadence the typical green sludge was not. Though, had Caspian offered her barrels of green sludge, she would have sucked it down to fill the hole in her belly.

The unseen rise of his brow colored Caspian's question. "Did you not feed her?"

A deadpan, was offered in reply. "I fed her often."

Even with warm food in her mouth, a chill crept up Wren's spine at Kieran's tone.

Swallowing the food stuffed in her cheeks, she reached for a folded napkin, wiped her hands, and turned around.

"Keep eating, mouse." Even moderate, there was something under Caspian's order. "And don't forget your dessert under the silver dome."

Both males were watching her in very different manners, Wren's eyes darting from one to the other. Caspian was calculating, lounging in his chair. Kieran was ominous, staring at her as he was wont to do.

Still hungry, Wren hesitated. That was when she looked past her own discomfiture to notice the room. It was more than the table laden with fine cuisine. It was the stale nature of the place.

It was the bed adorned with the finest nest she'd ever built—still intact. A nest she had enjoyed for less than an hour before she'd been paraded in front of Caspian's men and made to watch Toby beat her boy bloody.

No one had touched it. No other female scent wafted under the delicious aromas emanating from the table.

Caspian had not despoiled her nest or this room the entire time she'd been gone.

Their eyes met, the male neither addressing what must have been a question on her face, nor challenging her appraisal.

He wanted her to look at him.

Free of his coat, cheek freshly shaven, commanding, male, and powerful. Seated, so they were of equal height.

Familiar.

"Eat." How Caspian managed to drench one gently spoken word with so much arduous command, she'd never know.

Wren wanted to eat his food, not solely because she hungered, but because instinct commanded she take the male's offering.

A beautiful offering of more than sustenance. An offering she had taken for granted, stuffing it into her mouth with her fingers like she had.

It had not been appreciated or fully recognized.

So she did it now, savoring a moment so rare.

A single place setting waited.

Fork, knife, spoon, silver-rimmed bone china plate.

There was even creamy linen. Had the table boasted flowers and candlelight, it would have been straight out of an old painting.

Fingertips brushing the crisp fabric, Wren hummed, mind full of the wonderful dress she could make out of this panel. It wouldn't last five minutes in the squalor of the Warrens, but for those brief, pristine moments, it would have been grand.

Better than her dress made from fancy, old curtains.

Lifting the waiting plate in careful fingers, the smoothness of china, the fact there wasn't a single crack or chip was marvelous. So clean she could see herself in it, it was turned so the light might play off the sheen.

Plenty of times during salvage she'd come across old, cracked remnants of some long dead person's fine dishes.

Some with painted flowers or intricate designs.

But this simple bone china with light detail and a high polish—this was prettier by far. Though it would have been frivolous and held no true value in the Warrens, she would have snatched it from whatever lair she'd haunted and kept it in her box of treasures.

Her boys would not have been allowed to touch it.

Before she realized what she'd done, the plate was cradled to her breast, realization that her box of treasures was buried so deep under the mud that it would never be salvaged, spoiling her joy.

An impatient male noise at her back, and Wren lost the far off look in her eyes, cheeks stained with an embarrassed flush.

Setting down the dish, a sheepish twist to her mouth, she signed to Caspian. *It's very pretty*.

"Spell out what you just said."

She did, brows drawing together to find that he was actually paying attention to her hands.

It took a moment, before Caspian strung the gestures into meaning, but he did. He'd learned her alphabet. "Pretty."

And she was all shock, nodding, fairly certain the expression on her face was laughably stunned.

26

Pasta in enough cream sauce to drown a rat. When Wren had taken the time to pay attention to the offerings, that was what her shaking hand reached for.

Noodles drenched in heaven.

It had been years, *years*, since she'd eaten anything nearly this frivolously decadent. Real cheese, real cream, from real cows. Nothing powdered, and by the texture, she imagined the linguini was handmade and fresh.

The kind of dish served upstairs to smiling patrons of restaurants. Something that required silverware, both spoon and fork.

At first, it was awkward spinning the noodles in the bowl of the spoon, and she knew she looked absolutely ridiculous to the two males who refused to give her the privacy to stuff her face properly. Both stared, both occasionally offering a grunted and pointless noise when she moaned over the perfect bite.

Alec would lose his mind for this, would slop the tureen of pasta up to his mouth and drink it dry. Her other ward, Mikael, would be head over feet for the whole fish dressed with actual lemons.

Considering there was more than enough for ten men waiting on the table, it was a shame she couldn't share it with them. Deep down, a part of Wren wanted to be bitter; the tired woman who missed her boys itching to rebel against the very Alphas measuring her every bite. The wiser part of Wren told her to remember that Alec was up top and Mikael was still getting treatment. And that was the best she could do in this moment.

There would be *other moments* she would steal for them later.

Someday, if she survived this, she might actually be able to prepare a meal this delicious for her boys.

The thought made her smile around a dripping bit of linguini.

The males noticed, each reacting with a noise that broke the spell the food had created.

Feeling a dollop of cream sauce at the corner of her lips, Wren chewed the noodles, looking from Caspian to Kieran and back again.

She wanted to eat more, to truly gorge until it hurt, but Caspian had not done this for her pleasure. He'd done it for his. A groggy female too full to fuck him would lead her to trouble, so Wren pushed the plate away with a sigh, wiped her mouth, and rose from her chair.

"Dessert, little mouse." Caspian's eyes went to the waiting silver dome, urging the Omega to reach out and grasp the lid.

Having never been much of a fan of sweets, Wren obeyed, disinterested and full enough. Except the dome was stuck, an odd weight behind the curved metal. Tugging, bearing more of her weight against it, it gave, the clatter, the overflow of what was inside more jarring than the heft of the lid.

The silver dome lid hit the floor when her hands failed, when her heart stopped. The clang and resounding bell-like vibration made an ugly sound, the opposite of a purr. One that blended with the *tink* of credit chips spilling over.

She'd backed to the wall, shoulders to her ears at the crumbling display, and felt as if she wouldn't be able to draw breath.

Never in her life had she seen so many credit chips, some in denominations she didn't imagine existed.

Carrying even a handful of this in the Warrens would see her throat slit ear to ear.

Her friendliest neighbors would murder her for even one.

Knowing it was ridiculous to feel such terror for inanimate objects, unable to control her panting or to look away from the tumbling pile, Wren began to slowly inch away.

Shoulder blades scraping along the wall, she edged closer and closer to the door.

Still the chips slid over one another, their momentum slowing, which only made the *slink* and *clicks* all the more precise.

As she stared at that crumbling pile, Kieran growled, "What's wrong with her?"

"She's frightened." And Caspian no doubt felt it through their link, surprised enough that it shaded his response. "You came back to demand payment, mouse. There it is. Take it. It's yours."

Pockets full of coins, he'd said. Enough water for a year. That pile of cash was beyond money for bribes. That pile of cash would be a target on her back if anyone knew she had it. She couldn't even carry it all. And she had no idea what it was actually worth outside of her personal hellhole.

Too much, she was certain.

"Payment?" Kieran spat, snide and every ounce the arrogant male she had first met. "You claimed you came for your boys. You lied to me, female."

Kieran's unexpected anger was so far off her

radar, that Wren ignored him completely, even while skirting her body behind his—as if he might stand as sentinel against an inanimate pile of credit chips.

Aware she was acting like a lunatic, but unable to stop herself, she wrung her hands.

Warm, yet brokering no argument, Caspian declared, "It's yours. Consider our bargain fulfilled. You stay here, your boys get that. No sulking, no sad faces. I own you fully."

It all sounded so reasonable, which stirred up her adrenaline all the more.

These were not reasonable men. Caspian had only ever lied to her, stolen her child, had him beaten, used her body, marked her without permission.

And that very male was rising out of his chair, unfolding slowly to his full, massive height.

Still the pile of credit chips was far more daunting.

All that food sat like a weight in her belly, churning with her heart until Wren felt sweat gather at her temples. The last unbalanced chip fell from the pile, that horrible music over, and lavender eyes broke away to fall, lost, on the approaching First.

Signing, aware she was completely ridiculous, she asked. *"What do I do with it?"*

"You'll have to write it down, mouse." Just like

the slate she'd used in her lost home to speak with him, Caspian produced a panel and chalk.

An entire piece of unbroken, unused, precious chalk.

She wrote down her question, the male ignoring the stink of anger wafting from Kieran as he answered. "You sold yourself to me. I don't care what you do with it."

Mikael could go to school like a normal kid. He could sleep above the filth and dirt. He wouldn't have to scavenge or steal. Alec could rule the world with that pile of sin.

"You won't take it away?"

Pulling Wren from where she'd wedged herself between the wall and the Second, Caspian said, "Kieran, leave the room. Go to the pen, fuck off the rut, and deal with your new mate before I get another complaint."

Clenched teeth, sporting real, acrid rage. "This bitch told me she returned for her boys."

Caspian cocked his head, eyes narrowed. "She did. The money is for the boys." Putting a hand to Wren's shoulder, his next words were for her. "And there won't be any further hard feelings. Isn't that right, Jax?"

Her heart was bursting with hard feelings, chalk dashing over slate so she might scratch out her growing fear, *"I still need to see them."*

Large fingers pinched a lock of white hair, mud-brown eyes indulgent as he toyed. "On occasion, unless you give me reason to refuse. Try to run, hide from me, and I'll make sure you never see your boys ever again. You are bought and paid for now. No more negotiations."

Coming back to the Pipeworks had been a death sentence after all.

She would die here. Just not today.

Meanwhile, her boys would have a real chance, not that she wanted to approach, touch, or horde that pile of wealth that would secure it for them.

"It's only money, girl."

Only money? That was a life sentence combined with an actual chance for survival. It was beyond comprehension to someone who'd never had more than ten credits in her hand *ever*.

"You were supposed to be grateful."

She might not get murdered in the Warrens for that pile of money, but lifting that silver dome—the one that was no doubt dented from the fall—was the death of her. This was it, *really it*.

Her body had been sold for tangible payment, and it felt far more weighty than any claiming mark.

Forehead settling to Caspian's chest, drawing in the scent of him, seeking comfort from the jabbing blend of feeling, Wren closed her eyes to all of it.

Stroking her hair, Caspian offered a light purr,

neither overly indulgent nor manipulative. It was just there, like his heartbeat was there.

Without the weight of terrible threat hanging over her children, the exchange felt different. More normal.

Even natural.

But only a fool would let herself enjoy it. It could be days, it could be months, but Caspian would find another new girl to trick, spoil, and fuck. He would get bored of a complacent, damaged Omega.

Lashes lifted, one final breath of perfect Alpha, and Wren sold her dreams for the bright future of her boys. With a smile, she pulled back, held out her hand, and struck a bargain with a veritable monster.

It wasn't a handshake the male sought to seal their deal. Lips brushing hers, he murmured. "Good girl."

27

S ilk. Spider silk as pale as moonlight caught Caspian in a web he'd gladly tangle around his limbs. Around his cock. Fuck, it would feel incredible stroking his cock.

Running over his hips while he pushed her head down his shaft.

Their last mating had been vulgar in its transience. One frenzied thrust before the knot he'd fought to produce for a goddamn week burst forth. Flooding her so soon had left the taste of heaven on his tongue, even if she had been coated in filth, and stinking of sickness.

Tasting her now, blood pumped into an overly swollen cock, the teeth of his zipper barely contained what pulsated and wept. Had Rosie's lips been stretched around such girth as Caspian had watched the pretty mouse eat, he would have cum each time the female sighed. He would have broken Rosie's jaw with his knot when the mouse moaned.

As it was, an astonishing amount of fluid had built up in his sack. It felt as if it sloshed when he pressed closer to his greatest treasure, that it churned. Had his pants not held back his prick, it would have bounced with each pulse of blood in his veins.

He was going to hurt his mouse. There was no stopping it.

Not after the hours Caspian had let build between them. Not after her sweet sighs over the feast he'd provided.

For two full days Kieran had been allowed to keep her despite neglecting his duties.

For good reason. Caspian wanted *his* mouse to be grateful to return to her true owner, her *First* owner. He wanted to measure her expression of relief when the handsome one no longer had first claim.

It was so rare a victory Caspian might lord over his Second.

Mission accomplished. Kieran reeked of covetous agitation and his mouse had indeed arrived no longer wearing the betrayal that had pinched her brows when last he'd been buried in her.

Two days with the cruelest of them had washed

her clean of her animosity, but not of Kieran's scent… or the Second's terrible choice in clothing.

That fucking dress covering his mouse was the stuff of nightmares. Where Kieran had even found a garment like that down here, Caspian could only imagine. His whores sure as hell didn't sport matronly shit.

This was the costume old mated Alphas demanded their Omegas wear in public. The dress of a wife who was to be acknowledged but not physically appreciated by others. Breeding Omegas only displayed their beauty for their mates.

If it was a joke, Kieran lacked the quirk to his smile usually accompanying his tricks. Instead his body language was aggressive—fists balled, jaw clenched, his green-eyed glare on the female obediently allowing Caspian the feel of her mouth.

Until that covetous gaze drifted to where Caspian stared right back at him, even while sampling the parted lips of his mouse.

Fingers slipping to cradle the back of her skull, Caspian played the gentle lover a few moments longer, measuring the Second's reaction. Amazed, he found blatant challenge in his subordinate's low, unguarded growl.

Breaking from kiss-reddened lips, from an enticed female bearing half-conquered slowly expanding pupils, the First met the unspoken challenge. "Kieran?"

"I'll watch." Gruff, lacking all proper deference, his Second widened his stance.

After delivering her still reeking of Kieran's cum, there was no fucking way such behavior would be rewarded.

Hell, even Toby had been removed from the equation for this calculated reunion—sent off with the perfect prey. Down in the bowels of the pipeworks, the Third was creaming his pants tormenting the instigator of a sorry power grab.

The failed assassin would be an interesting corpse to view once the Third was done with him—for aside from the sweet scent wafting from the slickening pussy before him, Toby's greatest joy lay in well-thought-out torture.

Acquiescing when Caspian drew her head to his chest, his mouse inhaled deeply, nosing his chest in the exact way he both adored and despised. Flawless female submission before Kieran, her obvious enjoyment of his scent—despite any unpurged anger—led Caspian to smile.

His rugged, scarred face, the wrinkles collected at the corners of his eyes, she preferred him anyway. And she always had.

Always would.

This Caspian broadcasted in the meanness of his grin. In the blatant demand of his glare.

At her little noise once his scent hit the back of her throat, another wave of backed up seed inflated his sack, threatened to break down his cock. Caspian growled, dominant, virile, and already lost completely to the rut. "Leave."

There was a reason Kieran held the rank of Second. He was not one to be fucked with. "I hold second claim."

Cock twitching, bleeding precum to the point his trousers and the Omega's belly were sticky with fluid, Caspian fisted the Omega's glorious hair. Baring her covered throat to his lips, he licked where her jaw met the unpierced lobe of an ear, watching his Second's every tick. "No one challenged that point."

Teeth clenched, eye twitching, Kieran stated a tired fact. "Our agreement was that I breed her in estrous."

"She's not in estrous." More importantly, there was a little doll made up to look like the mouse. A doll tucked away in the pen who'd make the breeding of another female impossible so long as she lived… unless she was in the room and made to participate.

No bonded Alpha could dump working sperm in another pussy. Kieran had to know that after these last days hording the mute Omega away. He'd probably had difficulty even knotting, grown frustrated with her.

Brow cocked, chin nuzzling the top of the silent mouse's head, Caspian added, "Toby refuses to allow other females near our mate. You'd have to kill the doll you paid for."

And there was always the fact that once Toby got his crack at the estrous high mouse, once he fully forged a pair-bond, his gushing prick would rinse out and destroy any defunct remnants left by another male. Kieran would not have his way in this. Not that he didn't deserve to be mocked for daring to deliver her cleansed and pristine.

"Done." Burning green eyes remained locked on Caspian, Kieran physically growing, drilling his attention on his leader, as he verbally ended the life of his doll.

Under Caspian's blatant caress, the mouse stiffened.

Another point won for the First, his game to seize her full and real attention far more fruitful than he'd imagined when he'd ordered the food and piled up a small fortune. "The doll is claiming pregnancy."

Considering Kieran's style had always been petulance, it had been some time since Caspian had seen his Second display this level of outright anger.

Running a hand through disheveled hair, snorting a huff of hot breath, Kieran barked, "The bitch wasn't in estrous. There is no pregnancy."

It wouldn't be so easy as that. "The rumor that you're about to add to your brood has already spread. The doll even demanded a place where Giggi and Oriella den with your other brats." Because the Second could never resist a bet, Caspian added. "One-million credits that you'll be clapped on the back when you leave the room. Half the Syndicate is waiting to congratulate you."

A pale, small hand reached to where Caspian held the mouse's hair in a tight fist. Stroking his fingers, she tried to urge release.

Distracted, breaking his eyes from the intruding male, mud-brown eyes cut to lavender. Her pupils had retracted, the female no longer in a state ready for mating. She was in a state for scolding—a thing he'd learned she could accomplish with a single look.

Had he been one of her boys, it may have worked.

He was not her child. He was her god.

He'd branded and paid for her, letting her know his thoughts with a lick of his lower lip and a growl.

The scent of slick as it gushed upon his call, softened the hard set of his eyes. The way she pressed her legs together as if she might hold it in, enthralling. "Do you have something to add, pretty mouse?"

Without preamble, her little palm cupped his erection.

And all hell broke loose.

It no longer mattered that a Second in need of a dry fuck up the ass lingered to watch. It no longer mattered that Caspian's intentions to woo her had been interrupted.

All that mattered was ripping open that hideous dress so he might lick the intoxicating fluid dripping down her thighs. Pound his strength into her slender body. Pour as much cum as possible into her womb.

Teeth itching with the need to clamp down and set his mark again, fabric split and fell away in ribbons with his enthusiasm.

And then he saw it... another male's still swollen mark on her neck.

28

With an arm snaked around the slight thing's torso, Caspian hauled the mouse's spent body into the perfect position so he might view where they were still joined. Pale ass up, her cheek to the mussed nest. Limp and exhausted and thoroughly branded, she let him do as he wished.

Kieran forced to watch and forbidden to participate.

Every muscle packed into Caspian's bulk seemed loose now that the last jettison of cum had spilled from his sack. And though the Omega's fist-tight cunt dribbled the occasional leak, so much of him was still inside her that there was no question who was master.

He was. He was *the* Alpha. First in the city—the

entire fucking planet if Caspian had his way. And *she*? She was his Omega to fuck, fill, and fondle at will.

Completely subdued now, the female did little more than twitch when he spread her ass cheeks wide to behold the glory of where the root of his cock was held tightly in her body.

The knot he'd pinned her with made a slow retreat, only large enough now to thin the skin around her well-fucked hole. Labia stretched when he slowly began to withdraw, knowing a flood waited behind that barrier, he teased his dick back enough that one minuscule, further movement would pop the seal and see him sprayed with what waited in her deluged channel.

"Your pretty pussy's blooming, naughty girl." Using his fingers, Caspian stretched her labia further, teasing her with stings that both hurt and pleasured. "Hold every drop when I pull out. If you spill any, you'll be punished."

An impossible feat.

The Omega was about to release a warm torrent that would drench his slick-shined thighs, coat the back of her legs, and puddle on the bedding. He'd roll her in it, work it through her hair. Force it between her lips. And punish her with another bite.

His teeth already itched, buzzed with the need to clamp down… again.

Eyes glazed in lust, Caspian pulled against her resisting vaginal opening, favored with a quick gush when she clenched to hold him from retreating so rudely.

"Already spilling my gift?" Dark, the growl working his voice into something animal, Caspian swiped a finger through the little trickle, zigzagging from her stuffed cunt and down her thighs. Bringing that sperm-laced sweetness to his lips, he sucked the digit clean with a loud pop. "Every drop you spill I'll shove right back in you, pretty mouse. You'll be corked with my cum, walk around with it sloshing in your belly until every cell in your body has my mark in it."

A spit-drenched finger circled her anus, threatening to push forward and breach.

Watching her involuntarily clench, knowing it would force out another splatter of cream from her cunt, he clicked his tongue. "I said hold it."

She was fucking flawless in her wide-eyed, blown pupil, haze. No matter his commands, her cunt *wanted* to keep all he threatened to let spill. It desired the very knot he was using to stretch and strain her opening.

Uptight scruples or not, the female fucking loved the exact way he wrecked her.

Considering how deeply he'd needed to fuck, he'd known he'd hurt her before the rut had fully destroyed his senses. By the state of her back—the myriad fresh bites and extensive bleeding scratches —he'd done actual damage.

But his female healed quickly, complained little, and had cum on his cock more times than any woman he'd fucked before. *And he'd fucked them all.* Any Omega, mated or not, that he'd desired. Betas by the truckload. He'd even mounted a raging, violent Alpha female or two.

Those battles and victories had been stimulating, but it was nothing to *this*.

This Omega? When pushed past the pale, she'd fought back exactly in a way the beast within craved. Tooth and nail, screams and grunts.

He too bled.

Having tempted her to mentally degrade and savage his body until Alpha blood filled her mouth. The same mouth now parted as the mouse tried to catch her breath. The sweet mouth that had kissed his lips, licked at the mark on his neck she's left all those weeks ago.

A place she had dared to bite him a second time at the cusp of his fifth or sixth climax.

Caspian had almost blacked out from the sheer force of his physical response to her sharp teeth. He'd roared and rammed when her nails gouged deep lines down his back. And when the manic fog had cleared, he had her over him, riding an engorged cock gone purple with blood, and found her taking her pleasure despite new bruises and wounds.

A pale head had been thrown back, inhuman noise coming from her throat as she milked his knot and ground her pelvis hard enough to make his groin ache.

The things he'd threatened her with for presuming to dominate him were beyond vulgar. All this he snarled while strumming the needy clit peeking from her hood. Leaning back, the Omega had spread the thighs banking his legs all the wider. Challenging him to follow through while chasing his thumb for more.

She'd cum so hard she'd sobbed.

So very pretty when she cried, his knot ballooned even larger, big hands reaching to pull the female to his chest so those tears might fall and mingle with his sweat.

In that moment, Caspian had wished she could speak.

A declaration perhaps that of all males, she preferred him most. Her body already spoke that truth—he'd watched her with both Kieran and Toby, and though she enjoyed being fucked by his pack, there was something between he and she that neither Second or Third could touch.

It fluttered like a caught bird in the fragment of the weak bond he could sense. Something *his*.

The pretty mouse hated him, that was true. But when they were joined, her abhorrence splintered. When he fucked her past the point of reason, it disappeared altogether.

Mud brown eyes still locked on the diminishing knot stretching her cunt, squeezing the parted cheeks of her ass, Caspian finally forced the seal.

The massive flood of cream that followed set him groaning, urged another, weak spurt to dribble from the slit of his overused cock, and left her shrinking pussy contracting on nothing.

Which only made her spill more.

Which meant she'd have to be punished.

Crawling over her to lick at the fresh bite on her neck, he growled. "Bad girl."

It was so brief he wasn't sure if his eyes betrayed him, but he'd swear those words left her smiling. He didn't have a chance to confirm it, not with Kieran rushing forward to push his spurting cockhead into her mouth, stroking himself to a full finish.

Cheeks flooded with cum, too startled to swallow the entirety of the flow, it spilled back over the shaft half hanging from her mouth. Dripping down the veined length to mat trimmed pubic hair, all that seed marked the nest, changing what had been the territory of one male to the territory of two.

Kieran, who had been forbidden to touch his

mouse today, who had jacked off in the corner for hours, coming in a sloppy mess on Caspian's floor as his eyes begged for relief, had disobeyed a direct order.

Body drained, sack shriveled and tight to his body, cock overly stimulated and attached to a male no longer eager to fuck, Caspian grew uncomfortably hard too soon—not out of lust, but out of the base need to subjugate an encroaching male.

He had Kieran by the throat before the Second finished spilling, met envy-green eyes and let the other Alpha male see every ounce of rage.

And then he fucked him, with nothing but the Omega's lingering slick to ease a brutal entry.

Right there. Right next to her.

For as long as it took for the bleeding Second Alpha to submit and know his place. When Caspian came, ramming deep down his ass, it was dry, felt like sand rushing, scraping his cock raw, and horrible.

The Omega had drained all his cum.

An Omega who was no longer in the nest.

In his frenzy to beat and best a heaving Kieran, the little mouse had vanished.

29

The pile of credit chips spilled across his den's floor made it impossible for Caspian to know just how much the mouse had snatched up before fleeing. Even with both of her tiny palms full, she wouldn't have enough to escape the city—it would take almost every last chip he'd offered her to purchase that kind of transportation. Dale City didn't let people out, not when it could continue to digest them. And first, she'd need to collect her raggedy boys.

But even a handful of that fortune would pay for her to hide for a few weeks, to see her fed.

Fuck!

Tearing at his hair, dick limp and stinging, he paced the length of his room and plotted just where to begin exacting revenge for this. First, Alec would die. Slowly and screaming.

Next, he'd have Mikael skinned. His youthful face would make fine leather to patch a worn bit of Caspian's coat.

Then the mouse would be made to slave. For him, every day. No further restraint on his end in the ways he chose to use her. He'd break her. Crush her like a squealing rat.

But first he'd break Kieran.

Burning glare cutting to where the Second slowly climbed to his knees, Caspian saw nothing but rage.

After all, the list of Kieran's sins was long—his recent disregard for Alpha hierarchy blatant. And had he not distracted Caspian with willful insubordination, the mouse would never have stood a chance of escape. Had Kieran not kept her to himself for so long, she wouldn't have grown so desperate.

Everything had been fine before he'd rammed his bursting member down the mouse's throat!

Unsure when Kieran's thick neck had come into his grip, the First Alpha crouched over his long-time *friend*, saw the red-faced Second's pain-glazed eyes bulge, and prepared to squeeze the life from the Alpha. "She's Gone!"

But his Second refused to die, fighting back with

renewed vigor that sent Caspian sprawling after a well-placed blow to the ribs.

Hoisting up his naked mass, the First rounded on his prey—only to find Kieran manically searching the mussed nest for the missing female.

Despite the damage to his face and throat, the Second snarled, "She wouldn't leave!"

Chest rising and falling, enraged, Caspian rolled his shoulders, ready to kill. "Was it worth it? Disobeying a direct order for a fucking blow job… that what you were doing to her in the big room for two days, drowning my mouse in cum until she struggled to breathe?"

"Who would replace me? Bjorn? You ready to share your mouse with him after you drag her back?" Wiping the blood streaming down his nose, Kieran curled his lip. Green eyes cut to the spilled money, the male shaking his head. "Besides, what are you going to buy her compliance with next? Murder her boys, she'll fight you until she's dead. You're sterile and Toby is fucking psychotic. Let me breed her. She has a baby, she'll do whatever you want until her dying day."

That one statement, and Kieran's purple, fully erect cock spilled on the floor. Spurts of creamy white, thicker than regular cum began to gum up and dangle like one long spit-string to the tacky puddle. Caspian finally noticed why the room smelled so strongly of the other male.

Wild-eyed, Kieran was beyond the rut. So beyond that Caspian wondered if the male even realized he'd just ejaculated nutrient fluid all over the floor. "What makes you think I'm sterile?"

The hissed response came too fast and too agitated. "Even Toby's got a brat. All of us knock one of the pen up eventually. No one rides the whores more than you."

This was too rich. Ugly smile growing, Caspian reached for discarded clothing and began to dress. "You have two choices. I kill you right now, replace you with Bjorn, and toss your corpse to the slaves for dinner. Or, you leave this room as you are, ass bleeding, and spend the rest of your rut fucking your doll until that crap stops oozing out of your dick and your brain turns back on. You want to breed a female, breed her. I'll be the one to put a baby in the mouse."

Clarity cut through Kieran's hormone driven madness. "We agreed I'd kill the doll."

Ah, but Caspian was First and his word was law. "Now you're going to keep the marked bitch. Forever." Fastening his pants, he added, "And get this room cleaned up and prepared. Once I bring her back, the mouse won't be leaving it again."

COLD CLARITY ENVELOPED his rage like an icy blanket. Caspian, all Alpha, pure killer, made his way from the waterworks to the upper levels. He traveled with no guard, more than willing to accept any challenges.

Not that a single soul would dare.

Hunting the mouse was a waste of time; she'd come to him… begging with her big, pretty lavender eyes wet with tears.

She'd cry as he murdered her boys.

And she'd be made to endure his face, his cock, and his temper until her dying day.

With Mikael bedridden, it took a single barked order to see the kid under a guard large enough to take down a city block. His cunning mouse would never get through that kind of firepower.

Leaving Caspian's obvious first target Alec. He'd have the slippery kid by the throat before he might get wind of her escape and hide.

Mikael would be left for seconds. Slow seconds, peeled while still breathing.

Yes, Kieran had made a good point. The mouse would be despondent once her wards were disposed of, but his Second had also lit upon the perfect chains. A baby.

Maybe several. An entire brood.

Images of her fat with his child, of her pale belly bulging and her breasts leaking milk, distracted.

Caspian made a mistake in offering the female money.

One single pile of money—a monstrous and outrageous sum—so much more than he'd ever paid for a single whore in the pen. A greater total than he'd paid for all of them together, wasted.

Money she must have realized, Alec would no doubt piss away the second he got cocky. After all, wealth, like power, required far more mental fortitude than most people understood. That was why so many men couldn't hold it; their minds couldn't wrap around the concept.

That was why the mouse had backed away in terror once she realized the gift he offered.

Truth be told, that was why he'd offered it. He'd known every last credit chip would have eventually ended up back in his pocket. But he'd been a fool to think she would return his kiss with more than obedience. Hate him as she might, he'd been so sure she'd still love him just enough for what this monetary reprieve would do for her wild children.

Caspian had been so sure.

Kieran would covet. Toby would maneuver. She would be settled between them. Each party playing their part.

Sharing her until they were bored, the pack

would thrive in its rivalries and hatreds as it always had. The Syndicate would prosper. Dale City would continue to bow.

Fawn over him… just as the missing mouse should have.

Fuck!

He'd had her cunt, he'd had her blood in his mouth, he'd had her defeat… her very life in his hands. But even with payment, he didn't have her at all.

But he would.

It would only take a matter of hours of having Alec's screams broadcast over the city's communication network before she came running right to his feet.

The lift carrying him to Dale City's finest residential district slowed, the doors before him parting until a warm breeze drifted over the steaming male. Sunshine, the sound of birds and carrying murmur of talking people filtered through.

None of it touched him.

Focused to a pinpoint, Caspian didn't so much as sneer at the crowd who recognized just what male had emerged into their midst. Scrambling away, some bowing in deference, a few actually pissing their pants when their eyes alighted upon his coat.

The streets cleared.

Not a single challenge.

Not one.

Not a single fucking soul dared so much as look him in the eye. Not a single guard dared question his advance through secured gates or lifts. Striding through the upper levels without guards and reeking of Omega cunt, Caspian smirked as the rich took one look at him, eyeballed his coat, and turned to flee. Dingy city streets became walled off, manicured lawns, Toby's sprawling family estate out of place in Dale City's gilded squalor.

Alec was ensconced within, one of dozens of nameless servants no one cared about.

As Caspian approached, the final door retracted, solid steel encased in stained oak millwork—the artifice reminiscent of bygone eras where wealthy assholes played croquet while their underlings labored their lives away.

It was fitting, really.

Nothing had really changed in hundreds of years.

Except now the rich had to pay him for every last drop of water they wasted chilling their fancy cocktails with ice. And that was a beautiful thing indeed.

The moment a servant was in sight, Caspian barked, "Bring me the boy, Alec."

Bent backed, bearing the wig worn by butlers the world over, the doorman was wise enough to not so much as twitch a nostril. "They await you in the master's quarters, great Alpha."

Entering the manse, heavy footfall hitting the mirrored floors, Caspian stopped short, barking. "What?"

The old man had to have been half deaf, his bent frame struggling to close the weighty doors. "Would you care for refreshment before you join the Master and his female?"

Unwilling to wait for the old codger to escort him forward, he brushed the old man aside—the butler caught by a waiting guard before he broke a hip on hard floors. Not that Caspian gave a fuck.

He didn't even notice with his brain twitching in his skull.

Because in that house, under the sparkling chandeliers and polished walls, lingered the scent of a well-fucked Omega.

One oozing the blended aroma of his cum and her slick.

The perfume was laced in blood, and peppered with agitation. And it was fresh, easy to trail, not that Caspian didn't know the exact layout of every room in the Third's family mansion. Not that he didn't have plants walking these ugly halls to spy on every last move the influential Ross family made.

Robotic, marching up the second half of a curved staircase, stomping down halls past startled servants and pointless attendants, he hunted that scent.

Past ancient artwork and Grecian statues, a fili-greed door was cracked. That sliver framed a seated female. One with clean, wet hair. One bathed in sunshine, a view of the city ignored as she sat motionless and stiff.

Clothed in a dove-gray housecoat, she stared at the far wall.

Sitting with a chair pulled to face the female, leaning his weight on his knees, Toby toyed with a damp strand of her hair. All the while, he spoke to her in a voice too low for Caspian to hear. He spoke to her without his manic grin, seemingly serious, yet unable to stop fingering that same white lock.

There was no nod, nor did she flat out ignore the male. The mouse *tolerated*.

And now that he'd gone quiet, Caspian could *feel* a shadow of what she felt. His mouse was angry and equally beholden toward Toby. *Not afraid, not frantic*—still as a glassy lake churning at its greatest depths.

Toby was oblivious to her internal turmoil—still murmuring, still closer than the female obviously was comfortable with.

Paused outside the door, stealing the view through that tempting crack, Caspian drank her in.

As if she sensed him, her head turned. Luminous

lavender eyes landed on mud-brown, Caspian slowly pushing the door wide.

Her lips, still pink from his recent attention, quirked into a small smile of greeting. And in that moment, Caspian felt his soul twist.

This was no runaway.

30

____

"Ungh..." God, there went another one—cum evacuating his balls, a full-body shiver sent Kieran's eyes rolling back. The chemical tension waned, a fulfilling knot partnered with a female who screamed in exactly the enthusiastic ecstasy he enjoyed best. And just when he thought the relentless rut might be over, the same need rushed right back in.

Sizzling nerves until orgasm turned into an extended, pained groan.

This pussy, it wasn't enough.

He'd always hated being told who he had to fuck, saddled with Caspian's leftovers when ordered to take the most recently used up bitch off his leader's hands.

Sure, those females were typically gorgeous,

well-trained, and willing—much more willing to suck his cock than they had ever been for Caspian. Publicly riding those bitches before The Syndicate had established Kieran's status as Second; knocking up a few who'd hated Caspian, most had even been fun.

But this one, she wasn't his castoffs. The First had not even accepted her as a gift, despite Kieran's expense and trouble. And though the doll's cunt felt spectacular and her scent was pure Omega, she'd never been more than something to play with.

And, of course, dressing her up had been a great dig at the boss—all that bleached hair and pale skin so close to Caspian's mouse.

This doll, the drooling girl whose pussy churned around Kieran's cock, should have placated the Second's need to fuck through this abnormal rut. It should have gratified him that she ultimately wasn't Caspian's castoffs, but it burned that he'd been ordered to drain his balls into a female.

He'd been ordered to *breed* her.

That wasn't their deal.

Jax was their deal.

Caspian got to mark and fuck an Omega he would not be required to keep once he grew bored. Estrous would hit, and Toby, despite the myriad reasons he shouldn't, would fully claim the Omega. Caspian would be free, Toby would get his forever plaything, and Kieran would be the first to fill her body with child.

Everyone got something.

And now, Caspian unsettled the balance, saddling him with a female who would not stop talking!

Even with his hands around her throat, she managed to squeak out, "I love you, Kieran."

Cock coughing up another round of abundant sperm, Kieran bucked, ignored the corresponding feminine squeal, and squeezed his swollen eyes shut. When she continued to bleat, his palm left her neck and pressed over her mouth.

The bitch must have liked it, because she came again, cunt encouraging his knot to throb and expand all the larger.

It was so skincrawlingly *intimate* like this, no matter how he tried to silence her. No matter if he mounted her from behind or made her wail. Twice he'd even caught himself staring at the bite mark on her shoulder and salivating for another nip.

Both times he'd been thinking of another woman.

One he had bitten—right on the neck, in parallel to Caspian's claiming mark.

One who he should be buried in right now, dumping all this jizz into her belly. Encouraging her body one step closer to the estrous that would see her fat with his baby.

The rut should have been slipping, but that one thought and he was back in another frenzy. Swinging his hips even though they were knotted, he worked that spasming pussy as if by sheer force of will would see a baby planted.

"How many days has it been?"

Snarling, throwing a rage-filled glare over his shoulder, Kieran found Toby indolently leaning against the door.

Two fucking days riding the doll without relief. "Get out!"

"You didn't appreciate my last update, huh?" With an exaggerated sigh, Toby pushed off the door and sauntered closer to the sweating couple. "I thought you'd like to see the look on her face while I licked her sweet pussy until she couldn't take it anymore."

The bastard and his *updates*…

While rutting over the doll, a fucking holo projection had lit up more than once with uninvited images of Jax—Caspian gently peeling off the pretty Omega's robe so he might admire the marks he'd left on her body. Unaware Toby had been documenting the moment, the First Alpha had fucking cleaned a female's wounds. Bandaged them, even healed the worst with equipment Toby already had waiting in that fucking mansion.

The First Alpha had tended a female.

It wasn't done! And it should have left Kieran livid for a very different reason.

The doll had seen the projection, she'd asked questions. She'd asked for marks just like that!

So he'd fucked her until she'd grown hoarse and shut up.

Breath fanning over the back of his neck, a light touch tracing down Kieran's spine, he heard Toby lower his zipper. "She asked me about you. More than once. Course, I lied."

Animal growl in his throat, hair dripping sweat and body smeared with Omega slick, Kieran refused to take the bait. Not even when the Third's finger traveled down the crease of his ass to rim the place they both knew Toby wanted to claim.

"I told her you were fine. She thought Caspian might have left you a corpse." The Third pressed closer, daring much. "She actually *wanted* to talk to you."

Teeth clenched together, knot and cum and his traitorous sack doing nothing to ease his need, Kieran hissed, "Fuck off, Toby."

The blunt head of a swollen shaft prodded his ass, threatening and tempting.

Feeling the male's hands grip his hips, offering

little more than token resistance, Kieran ignored the riled grunts of the woman neither male paid any attention to, and felt Toby began to stretch his way through his tender ring.

"I hate to do this without my sunshine here." As if he'd prepared it all, his cock half-buried in Kieran's ass, a new hologram lit up before them. A crisp recording of Caspian's mouse being fucked beyond a measure of sanity.

Wrapped up in Caspian, Toby at her back, she was wild and beautiful, and glowing in the sun.

Under his palm, Kieran heard an indignant snarl from the doll, and barked at the interruption. "How many times do I have to tell you to BE QUIET!"

Slick easing his entry, Toby bottomed out, purring at Kieran's ear. "Do you see her? Last night she took us both at the same time. You could have been in her mouth." Hands rounding his waist to grip the exposed root of Kieran's cock, Toby hummed, "You could have drained this dick down her throat."

Meat jerking where it was buried in Omega pussy, knot pulsating—not from an annoyance, but in a very real manifestation of pleasure—Kieran groaned at the fantasy. More than cum drained from him, and it had little to do with the way Toby dragged his girth over Kieran's prostate.

A familiar Omega call blasted over the room's

speakers left him pressing back, dragging the thing attached to his dick with the movement. Caspian's mouse couldn't have known that Toby had recorded her, she never would have cried out like that had she the slightest inkling. From everywhere, audio cranked high, Jax's noises bounced around the room —a beautiful song punctuated by male grunts and the vicious snarls of Alphas taking what was theirs.

What was Kieran's.

Toby scythed in and out, jerking his hips hard enough to threaten a stretched anus with a budding knot. "Think of how she tastes, how tight her cunt squeezes down when you thrust in."

'Fuck!" A wave of raw sensation churned from Kieran's toes and fingertips, rushing forward through a system overly taxed by a disjointed rut. "Don't stop!"

Under him something squirmed, little teeth biting the heel of his palm. But Kieran didn't notice. There was a cunt around his knot, one no longer squeezing down as it should—a disembodied female presence so beneath his notice in that moment, that when he bent double, hands framing the complaining woman's body, it was as if she wasn't even there.

How could he pay her any attention while Toby hit that perfect spot?

Voice thickened by his own pleasure, the Third

took a firmer hold of Kieran's hips. Each word punctuated by withdrawing to the tip, and fucking in full force. "She. Wants. You. Back."

There was nothing more his sack could offer, Kieran cumming dry in a painful last lurch that felt so excruciatingly right.

Lips fell to his neck, Toby groaning out the beginnings of a release. Flooding Kieran's colon until his bowels ached.

There was the suck of a kiss on sweat-salted skin, the Third showing mercy by pulling out to spray the remainder of his spend on Kieran's buttocks.

Still buried in the flailing woman who reeked of anger, the Second could do little more than pant and keep his eyes locked on the projection.

Asshole leaking cum down his thigh, burning from misuse in a way that sent his skin to pebble, at long last his erection began to retreat.

The rut was finally broken.

Licking a flat-tongued trail to the shell of Kieran's ear, Toby whispered, "Don't give Caspian a reason to be jealous, and you won't get sent to the pen like the hypocrite you are."

The insult registered slowly, Kieran focused on the slither of his flaccid dick out of a slick vomiting channel. It registered just as the pain in his palm registered.

He was bleeding from a deep-set bite wound on his hand that was far more incensing than the psychotic Third's slander. About ready to break the aggravating female's neck, he shouted, "Did you fucking mark me?"

The wide-eyed doll scooted back like a kicked puppy, and for once, wisely kept her mouth shut.

Laughing, Toby ran his fingers over a similar, cum stained bite mark decorating Kieran's ass—one Jax had left there when she'd fought them in the waterworks before the Syndicate. "Now there's the ticket! Show that little beauty to Caspian, and he'll let you back between our mate's thighs."

Turning his back on the Omega, Kieran faced off against the Third.

Up to his disgusting tricks, Toby continued to grin and stroke his cock, denying his knot so it might grow ghastly. "Caspian is not going to let you do that shit to her again."

"Ahh." Toby let a dribble of cum splatter the floor as his poor knot began to creep down his shaft. "But I was a good boy and gave the boss several days to play with my sunshine. I followed orders… and tonight *I get my turn*. I intend to make the most of it."

The hologram shut off, the room going silent. "Caspian won't allow it."

"Caspian won't know. Sunshine is a good girl. She knows what to keep to herself."

Warning dousing his tone in pure grit, Kieran shook his head. "Toby…"

Changing the topic, it seemed the Third had final words of wisdom to offer. "He doesn't want Jax to like you. He sure as fuck does not want you to like her. That's where you made your mistake. For now, all her affection needs to be his. If she so much as smiles at you bigger than she smirks at him, I'll be getting a promotion I don't want. Don't go dumping more nutrient substance down her throat… at least where he can see. You get caught up in the rut again, you take it out on your doll."

The doll in question squared her shoulders and found her voice. "I'm his mate."

Unhinged smile growing, Toby gave her a wink. "My mistake, sweet cheeks."

And with that, he tucked away his still hard cock, and left the room.

When she reached out to stroke his arm, Kieran shook her off. Naked, he followed his friend, ready to bathe and get back to work.

LEFT ALONE AND STILL REELING, the doll sat in the nest she'd made special for her new love. It smelled of the perfect, most handsome male she'd ever seen. It was wet with his seed.

She'd done well!

But she had not done enough.

Another male's stink wafted from the scattering of his still-warm ejaculate. A series of tiny puddles left to befoul her blankets.

Toby... the Third ranked Alpha of The Syndicate.

Scooping some sticky, foreign spend on her fingers, the doll stretched Toby's cum between forefinger and thumb, watching the string snap while she considered.

A lick.

It didn't carry the same sweet flavor as Kieran's generous outpouring. More tangy, laced with underlying saltiness.

Pushing some up her cunt to see if it left her warm and tingling like Kieran's did, she felt nothing but the sore stretch of a raw pussy when her fingers kissed her cervix.

"You need to clear out of the room; the other girls need it." That bitch Rosie marched in, daring to issue orders... again.

Pulling her hand from her swollen sex, the doll answered back in the same imperious tone. "This is my den."

Rolling periwinkle blue eyes at the ceiling, the

blonde Omega sighed. "Do I need to call the guard again? They never take well to having to correct pen sluts. Just get up—" Rosie froze, nose twitching. Gaze dropping to where the doll sat with her legs splayed, she tripped over her question. "Did Toby? It smells like he…"

Brows tight with mistrust, doll stopped pouting to pay close attention.

"You know what, never mind." Rosie held her hands up, waving off the intrusion. "I'll have the girls use another room. This one's all yours."

Scoffing, doll got to her knees, a protective posture over a nest she'd be damned to abandon. The other woman must have thought she was pretty dumb to fall for it. "That's right. It's *mine*."

Pulling the sperm laden blankets to her chest, hoarding them close with a smile, she made sure to rub as much of the cooling mess into her skin as she could. Coated with the perfume of her mate, while also stinking of the cum of the Third, she stood from the bed, naked body on display.

Walking right past the wary blonde, doll marched straight into the pen for every last female and male to see and smell.

When eyes began to land on her and more whores' nostrils flared with the same tiny twitch Rosie's had, she put a hand to her hip and cooed, "Someone get me something to eat. I'm hungry."

And someone fucking did.
Doll ate well that night.

Thank you for reading SILENCED. I hope you loved Wren and the Alphas who've claimed her! Ready for more? Sign up for my newsletter ❧at addisoncain.com for the latest news on the next installment of Wren's Song.

**Craving More? Turn the page for a taste of
BORN TO BE BOUND**

Born to be Bound

Alpha's Claim, Book One

She watched him bolt the door with a rod so thick it dwarfed her ankle, trapping her, cornering the Omega for mating. Unsure if Shepherd had heard, she used her feet to scoot away from the male until her back hit the wall, and tried again. "Food… we can't go out... hunted, forced. They're killing us." Her blown pupils looked up at the intimidating male and pleaded for him to understand. "You are *the* Alpha in Thólos, you hold control... we have no one else to ask."

"So you foolishly walked into a room full of feral males to ask for food?" He was mocking her, his eyes mean, even as he grinned.

The horror of the day, the sexual frustration of her heat, made Claire belligerently raise her head and meet his eyes. "If we don't get food, I'm dead anyway."

Seeing the female grimace through another cramping wave, Shepherd growled, an instinctual reaction to a breeding Omega. The noise shot right between her legs, full of the promise of everything she needed. His second, louder grumbled noise sang inside her, and a wave of warm slick drenched the floor below her swollen sex, saturating the air to entice him.

She could not take it. "Please don't make that noise."

"You are fighting your cycle," he grunted low and abrasive, beginning to pace, watching her all the while.

Shaking her head back and forth, Claire began to murmur, "I've lived a life of celibacy."

Celibacy? That was unheard of... a rumored story. Omegas could not fight the urge to mate. That was why the Alphas fought for them and forced a pair-bond to keep them for themselves. The smell alone drove any Alpha into a rut.

He growled again and the muscles of her sex clenched so hard she whined and curled up on the floor.

It was hard enough to make it through estrous locked in a room alone until the cycle broke, but his damn noise and the smell invading past the rotting stickiness of her clothing was breaking her insides apart.

The degrading way he spoke made her open her eyes to see the beast standing still, his massive erection apparent despite layers of clothing. "How long does your heat typically last, Omega?"

Shivering, suddenly loving the sound of that

lyrical rasp, she clenched her fists at her sides instead of beckoning him nearer. "Four days, sometimes a week."

"And you have been through them all in seclusion instead of submitting to an Alpha to break them?"

"Yes."

He was making her angry, furious even, with his stupid questions. Every part of her was screaming out that he should be stroking her and easing the need. *That it was his job*! With her hand still pressed over her nose and mouth, her muffled, broken explanation came as a jumbled, angry rant, Claire hissing, "I choose."

He just laughed, a cruel, coarse sound.

Omegas had become exceptionally rare since the plagues and the following Reformation Wars a century prior. That made them a valuable commodity which Alphas in power took as if it was their due. And in a city brimming with aggressive Alphas like Thólos, she'd been trapped in a life of feigning existence as a Beta just to live unmolested, spent a small fortune on heat-suppressants, and locked herself away with the other few celibates she knew when estrous came. Hidden in plain sight before Shepherd's army sprung out of the Undercroft and the government was slaughtered, their corpses left strung up from the Citadel like trophies.

Claire had been forced into hiding the very next day, when the unrest inspired the lower echelons of population to challenge for dominance. Where there had been order, suddenly all Thólos knew was anarchy. Those awful men just took any Omega they could find; killing mates and children in order to keep the women—to breed them or fuck until they died.

"What is your name?"

She opened her eyes, elated he was listening. "Claire."

"How many of you are there, little one?"

Trying to focus on a spot on the wall instead of the large male and where his beautiful engorged dick was challenging the zipper of his trousers, she turned her head to where her body craved to nest, staring with hunger at the collection of colorful blankets, pillows—a bed where everything must be saturated by his scent.

An extended growl warned, "You are losing your impressive focus, little one. How many?"

Her voice broke. "Less than a hundred... We lose more every day."

"You have not eaten. You're hungry." It was not a question, but spoken with such a low vibration that his hunger for *her* was apparent.

"Yesss." It was almost a whine. She was so near to pleading, and it wasn't going to be for food.

The prolonged answering growl of the beast compelled a gush of slick to wet her so badly, she was left sitting in a slippery puddle. Doubling over, frustrated and needy, she sobbed, "Please don't make that noise," and immediately the growl changed pitch. Shepherd began to purr for her.

There was something so infinitely soothing in that low rumble that she sighed audibly and did not bolt at his slow, measured approach. She watched him with such attention, her huge, dilated pupils a clear mark that she was so very close to falling completely into estrous.

Even when Shepherd crouched down low, he towered over her, all bulging muscle and musky sweat. She tried to say the words, *"Only instincts..."* but jumbled them so badly their meaning was lost.

Starting with the scarf, he unwound the items that tainted her beautiful pheromones, purring and stroking every time she whimpered or shifted nervously. When he pulled her forward to take away the reeking cloak, her eyes drew level with his confined erection. Claire's uncovered nose sniffed automatically at the place where his trousers bulged. In that moment all she wanted, all that she had ever wanted, was to be fucked, knotted, and bred by that male.

Only instincts...

Shepherd pressed his face to her neck and

sucked in a long breath, groaning as his cock jumped and began to leak to please her. He had gone into the rut, there was no changing that fact, and with it came a powerful need to see the female filled with seed, to soothe what was driving her to rub against her hand in such a frenzy.

The words were almost lost in her breath, "You need to lock me in a room for a few days..."

A feral grin spread. "You are locked in a room, little one, with the Alpha who killed ten men and two of his sworn Followers to bring you here." He stroked her hair, petting her because something inside told him his hands could calm her. "It's too late now. Your defiant celibacy is over. Either you submit willingly to me where I will rut you through your heat, or you may leave out that door where my men will, no doubt, mount you in the halls once they smell you."

Read Born to be Bound now!

ADDISON CAIN

USA TODAY bestselling author and Amazon Top 25 bestselling author, Addison Cain's dark romance and smoldering paranormal suspense will leave you breathless.

Obsessed antiheroes, heroines who stand fierce, heart-wrenching forbidden love, and a hint of violence in a kiss awaits.

For the most current list of exciting titles by Addison Cain, please visit her website: addisoncain.com

facebook.com/AddisonlCain

bookbub.com/authors/addison-cain

goodreads.com/AddisonCain

ALSO BY ADDISON CAIN

Don't miss these exciting titles by Addison Cain!

Standalone:

Swallow it Down

Strangeways

The Golden Line

The Alpha's Claim Series:

Born to be Bound

Born To Be Broken

Reborn

Stolen

Corrupted

Wren's Song Series:

Branded

Silenced

The Irdesi Empire Series:

Sigil

Sovereign

Que (coming soon)

Cradle of Darkness Series:

Catacombs

Cathedral

The Relic

A Trick of the Light Duet:

A Taste of Shine

A Shot in the Dark

Historical Romance:

Dark Side of the Sun

Horror:

The White Queen

Immaculate

www.ingramcontent.com/pod-product-compliance
Lightning Source LLC
Chambersburg PA
CBHW021308190726
48288CB00003B/740